"A ROLLICKING STORY . . . FAST AND FUNNY."
—*USA Today*

"*HIS GRAND FINALE IS A TABLOID DREAM.*"
—Pete Hamill, *The New York Times Book Review*

"AUTHENTIC SIGHTS, SOUNDS, AND SMELLS OF THE NEWS BUSINESS . . . and a revealing insight into journalism, politics, and life on the not-so-far-out fringe."—Hal Bruno, Political Director, ABC News

DWARF RAPES NUN; FLEES IN UFO
Arnold Sawislak

"A GOOD, FAST READ . . . knowingly crafted by an author who knows his way around a newsroom."
—*John Barkham Reviews*

"A LOAD OF LAUGHS . . . LITERALLY TO THE LAST PAGE!"—UPI

"GO WITH IT! . . . JUST THE INCISIVE, IRREVERENT, HILARIOUS RESPONSE today's homogenized, tabloidized, chain-linked newspapers need and deserve. It is newsroom shoptalk at its profane best."
—John McCormally, Harris Newspapers

QUANTITY SALES

Most Dell Books are available at special quantity discounts when purchased in bulk by corporations, organizations, and special-interest groups. Custom imprinting or excerpting can also be done to fit special needs. For details write: Dell Publishing Co., Inc., 1 Dag Hammarskjold Plaza, New York, NY 10017, Attn.: Special Sales Dept., or phone: (212) 605-3319.

INDIVIDUAL SALES

Are there any Dell Books you want but cannot find in your local stores? If so, you can order them directly from us. You can get any Dell book in print. Simply include the book's title, author, and ISBN number, if you have it, along with a check or money order (no cash can be accepted) for the full retail price plus 75¢ per copy to cover shipping and handling. Mail to: Dell Readers Service, Dept. FM, 6 Regent Street, Livingston, N.J. 07039.

DWARF RAPES NUN; FLEES IN UFO

by Arnold Sawislak

A DELL BOOK

Published by
Dell Publishing Co., Inc.
1 Dag Hammarskjold Plaza
New York, New York 10017

Dell ® TM 681510, Dell Publishing Co., Inc.

ISBN: 0-440-12191-4

Reprinted by arrangement with St. Martin's Press

Printed in the United States of America

January 1987

10 9 8 7 6 5 4 3 2 1

WFH

FOR EMILE GAUVREAU,
who probably would have applauded

DWARF RAPES NUN; FLEES IN UFO

DWARF RAPES NUN; FLEES IN UFO

CHAPTER 1

The discussion, as I recall, was exploring one of your loftier points of editorial integrity when we got our first glimpse of the new management.

"The Garden Club election," Fargo said, "goes above the fold."

"You're joking, for Christ's sake," I yelled. "It's a society brief for Mary." When you get pulled off a nice, quiet statehouse beat to sit in "temporarily" as city editor, you figure you can yell a bit at the boss—at least a boss like Fargo.

Bill Grace, whose recurrence of shingles (or herpes if the girls in classified were to be believed) was responsible for my involuntary servitude in the office, claims he saw Fargo get mad once in eight years.

His wife sent him to work with a bean sprout and cream cheese sandwich, which Fargo bit into, gagged on, examined at length, rewrapped, and dropped into the Kapplan Brothers shopping bag he used as a briefcase. "Tastes like worms and toothpaste," he told Grace. "Looks like worms and toothpaste. Dumb woman."

I was not about to give up. "The goddamn officers were reelected, for Christ's sake," I yelled some more. "Three of them didn't even have opposition. It wasn't exactly Truman beating Dewey!"

"Front page," Fargo said, twining his fingers like a three-year-old learning to pray.

"Mrs. Morgan. That's why, isn't it? Fargo, you'd kiss the ass of a she-gorilla if she was a publisher's wife."

"It's their paper," Fargo said. "Give it a couple of inches and jump it to society. But it starts on the front . . . and above the fold."

If this had been a hypothetical situation in a journalism school exam, the right answer would have been: "A. Sir, I resign." In the editor's office in the only paper in town, if you have support and a car loan to pay and you've raised about as much hell as you figure you can get away with, the right answer is: "B. Shut up already and get back to work."

Which I started to do, when I almost collided at Fargo's office door with the gentleman whose wife had just made the front page of this afternoon's *Capital Register & Press* ("Fearless, But Friendly; Untouchable, But Understanding") with her remarkable and intensely newsworthy accomplishment of achieving a sixth term as treasurer of the town's petunia establishment.

J. Donald Morgan, sixty-two and not looking a day older than seventy-eight, nodded to me—I doubt he knew my name after only six years on the paper—and waved the Mutt and Jeff team behind him into Fargo's cubicle office.

It was late in the morning, which on a small town afternoon paper like the *CR&P* meant about 10:30. That day's paper was just about put to bed (somebody ought to do a Ph.D. thesis on the sexual overtones of newspaper jargon: "insert a graf," "hed to come," "hold for release," "boldface box"), and I was in charge of a nearly empty city room.

The paper's "crack news staff" (there we go again) consisted of sixteen full-time editors and reporters plus a couple dozen eager high-school kids who phoned in prep sports and hypersensitive little old ladies ("What do you mean, there's no space for the list of people who came to the church supper? I told *everybody* they would get their names in the paper") who mailed in badly typed or scribbled social notes from such teeming urban centers as Fenstermacher's Corners and Indian Crotch.

The Mutt character Morgan had in tow was a lean and

tweedy type with a face pocked by the memory of zits long healed and framed top and bottom with enough hair to do justice to a tea bag box. Everything about him seemed elongated; pipestem legs, a beaked nose sharp enough to slice cheese, fingers so long that they looked like they must have come equipped with a fourth joint.

Jeff was, to borrow the defiant self-description of a retired jockey I once interviewed, "well over four feet tall," a chunky Asian with a display of teeth worthy of a Steinway keyboard, and the biggest damn briefcase I've seen since my wife's lawyer came to court with affidavits from some of the ladies to whom I had somehow neglected to mention my marital status.

Morgan left Fargo's door ajar, and one of the handy-tricks-of-reporting-you-never-learn-in-journalism-school—don't eavesdrop unless you have a good hiding place—presented itself.

Fargo's office had a window looking into the nearly square low-ceilinged city room, which housed the entire editorial operation of the paper.

The creaky elevator from the first floor was in one corner and separated from the working area by a waist-high wooden railing. Next to the barrier were the two desks that dealt mostly with the public, sports, and society. State news had a desk off to one side near a row of filing cabinets and a reading table that were the paper's morgue. The local, national, and international news departments—the last two consisting of one editor and one teletype machine—had two desks and a table shoved together in the center of the room. I had one of the desks and my copyreaders (three, when things really got busy) had places at the table.

Opposite the state desk, the reporting staff had three desks off in a corner. Along the back of the room was a door leading to the photo darkroom and the window through which Fargo could keep his eye on this beehive of activity, but the door to his lair was on a side corridor. I suspected that was to quell any impulse by his staff to drop in to discuss such ugly subjects as pay increases.

This layout made it possible for me to move out of the line of sight of both Fargo and the staff and begin a careful examination of the water fountain in the corridor leading to the rear elevator. The water, as usual, was tepid. The audio was acceptable.

Morgan, in a voice as thin as a sheet of Zig Zag, said, "Ah, Mr. Barton . . ."

"Yes, *sir*, Mr. Morgan," Fargo replied in eager agreement. This established that Fargo knew and could respond to his own name, about which a lively debate could have been sustained in the city room, and that he recognized the publisher after only twenty-eight years on his payroll. A true triumph of corporate manuevering for Fargo.

"Mr. Barton, this is Mr. Shiu," Morgan said. "And this is Mr. Swift."

"Shigetsu Shiu," said the accented baritone voice I took to be the Oriental's. "Please to call me Shiggy."

"A pleasure, Mr. Barton," said the second voice, as high-pitched as any I have ever heard come from a man since Sam Darlington caught himself in his zipper.

Actually, it sounded like, "Play-shuh, stah-barn," but within weeks I was able to translate more or less simultaneously from what I am told is highborn English English into midwestern American.

Morgan again. "Mr. Barton, this is, ah, somewhat sudden, but, well, ah, there was no way to give you advance notice. There has been, ah, a change of ownership here at the paper. Mr. Shiu is your new, that is to say, he will be your publisher. . . ."

"Shiu? New?"

"Shiggy, Mr. Barton. Publisher, Mr. Barton," Shiu said, "And Mr. Swift, Mr. Granville Swift, is our new managing editor."

"New editor," Fargo said in a dead voice.

"No, Mr. Barton, managing editor. We would like you to remain as editor of the newspaper. Mr. Swift will deal with the news operation, and we would like you to preside over the editorial page—in consultation with myself, of course."

"Of course," Fargo said, with obvious relief at the prospect of a paycheck and a respectable climax to his career, taking pastel positions on such cosmic issues as the constitutional questions posed by the school board's imposition of dress code in the high schools.

Fargo was so relieved that it never occurred to him to ask what was to become of Morgan's brother-in-law Dudley, who held the title of editorial page editor and performed that function as perfunctorily as possible every weekday before he left for the country club.

Shiu told him anyway. "Mr. Graydon has elected to take early retirement and intends, I believe, to devote himself to his memoirs."

That struck me as downright remarkable, inasmuch as Dud Graydon was somewhere in his early forties, had never been farther from home than Chicago, and seemed unlikely to have much to write a memoir about—unless you count the time he wrestled a two-iron away from his golf partner when the guy tried to kill a goose that wandered on the course and honked just as he flubbed his sixth shot on the par three eighth.

"Nasty business," Dud told a circle of admirers in the clubhouse afterwards. "Even a goose has a right to express his or her opinion. After all, what else have we got to separate us from the damn communists? And Freddie was butchering the hole."

I was so engrossed by what was going down that I blew my cover. I stepped into the doorway of Fargo's office just as Shiu hoisted his balloon-sided briefcase onto the desk top. Fargo could see me but gave no indication; the others had their backs to me.

"My principals have instructed us to retain all of the present staff who care to continue in their current assignments for now," Shiu said. "However, Mr. Swift will be making some additions to the staff in several areas. Those need not concern you."

Shiu fished in the leather cavern on the desk and brought out a sheet of paper. "You will please print this notice in today's edition in a . . . ah, Mr. Swift?"

"A box," Swift said. "Front page, bottom right."

"But today's paper is already made up," Fargo said.

"Indeed?" Swift shrilled. "Then, Mr. Barton, let us consider Mr. Shiu's instruction to be your challenge for today. Get it in."

Shiu turned to leave—listing somewhat to the side he was carrying the briefcase—and then turned back to Fargo with a fluorescent smile. "And, Mr. Barton, perhaps it would be advisable for you to read the notice to the staff before sending it to the . . . ah, Mr. Swift?"

"Composing room," said Swift, following Shiu and Morgan past me without a flicker of interest. They disappeared into the elevator, presumably en route to the publisher's office upstairs.

Fargo got up, scanned the sheet of paper, and looked up at me. "Call the staff to the city desk."

"The staff" on duty consisted of me; Drew Claggett, who had been reading out advance feature copy that would be used to legitimize the potful of ads that had been sold for the annual June bride's special section; Mary Frasci and Doralee Green, the society page ladies who had been writing the slurpy copy for the section; Shep Carley, who had to hang around the wire until the press run began just in case World War III started before he could adjourn to Next Door— which was the bar next door; and Bicker, Snicker, and Whine, which is what everyone else called Al Wilks, the world's most cantankerous copyreader, Hank Terry, the sports writer who giggled at football injuries and racing car crashes, and Rip Tandee, who insisted he would have won a dozen Pulitzers if it had not been for the lousy camera equipment the lousy publisher bought for the lousy paper.

Fargo, who had seen pictures of this sort of drama ("Editor Reads News of Paper Folding to Staff") in *Editor and Publisher*, climbed up on a chair, cleared his throat and declaimed as follows:

"A NOTICE TO OUR READERS

"The *Capital Register & Press* today is being published under new ownership. *All-American Enterprises* of Chicago has acquired the property from the Morgan family and will continue to publish the newspaper as a unit of its extensive media and other commercial holdings in this country and abroad. Mr. J. D. Morgan has consented to remain with the company in a consultant capacity and Mr. L. Fargo Barton, the incumbent editor, will continue in that capacity.

"*All-American Enterprises* hopes and intends to bring to this community and to the state, whose government this city is the seat, a newspaper of the same unswerving distinction and high quality as was maintained by the former ownership. The new ownership also intends to provide an infusion of resources and innovative improvements to the property in order to assure its economic viability in the marketplace at large under the changing circumstances of today's requirements for maintaining an adequate level of profitability in both the near and far term.

"The new ownership wishes to assure the community that every effort will be made to continue, and we hope enhance the high standards of journalism and civic responsibility for which it has looked to the newspaper in the past. There will be some modernization of the newspaper's scope and broadening of its circulation base as a means of generating new revenues required to establish the property as a profit center that can occupy a proud place in the family of *All-American Enterprises's* entrepreneurial undertakings."

"Jesus," said Claggett. "The rag has been bought out by Philly lawyers." Drew was tough. He got that way reading *The Front Page* about twenty times.

"No, no," Mary said. "We've been swallowed by a multinational conglomerate. Arab sheiks, probably." Mary had saved her money and had a position in pork bellies. High finance was no mystery to her.

"The new publisher looks Oriental," I said.

"The Chinese Reds," Doralee announced, looking for all the world like a Roman virgin who has just spied Attila the Hun crossing the front yard. "Do they recognize marriage? Do they have spring proms?"

"Another paper about to go down the tubes," Bicker growled. "I give us three months with that kind of happy talk." Al had a loving wife, devoted children, and a host of friends who admired his untiring church and civic work. It wasn't until he came to work that he became a pain in the ass.

"Aren't we supposed to have a wake?" Shep asked. "I'll just go next door and get a couple of tables shoved together." Shep tipped a jar now and then. Actually, both now and then.

"Soccer. I bet they'll be apeshit about soccer. I don't know nothing about soccer," Snicker said, chuckling morosely. Hank had been a fair high school halfback and football was his passion. He regarded basketball as slightly sissified ("They play in short pants, f'Christ's sake") and liked nothing about baseball except collisions at home plate.

"I suppose this means there's no hope for getting a new enlarger," said Whine. Tandee actually was a pretty good photographer. It's just that nobody ever told him that except his mother.

Fargo turned to me with the notice. "This has to go in today as a front page box."

"No problem," I said, ignoring his obvious surprise at getting no argument from me. It took some shuffling, but we got the notice right where Swift wanted it. The only item that had to be spiked was the Garden Club election.

CHAPTER 2

The next month was quiet. Bill Grace, who dropped his drink and broke the glass on the new patio he had laid during his recuperation when he read about the paper being sold, made a miraculous recovery and returned to work, half expecting to find his city editor's job filled by some eager minion of *All-American Enterprises*. All he found was me, eager to get the hell out of his seat.

I went back to the pleasant and slow-paced environment of the fusty old statehouse pressroom, where I was bombarded with questions about what the hell was happening at the *Capital Register & Press*. Interest ran so high that the pressroom's perpetual low stakes hearts game was suspended while I was being interrogated.

"Who are these guys?

"Some big Chicago outfit. They say they have some other papers and some TV and radio stations."

"Which ones? Where?"

"I dunno. I couldn't find them in *Editor and Publisher*. But that's like looking for flyshit in pepper."

"What the hell do they want your paper for, Bob? Afternoon dailies are as useful as concrete bicycles. Why didn't they buy an A.M. paper?"

"I dunno that either. But they did get a monopoly, and I can't see anyone starting a morning paper here with the *Register* tying up all the good local ad contracts, and the rest of the gravy going to the dailies from the City and Chicago that can get here in time for morning home delivery. Maybe they're going A.M. with the *Register*."

"Oh, bullshit, Wartovsky. You haven't got five people over there that can either stay awake or stay sober past ten at night."

When it became clear that I really didn't know anything beyond what happened the first morning Shiu and Swift arrived, the hearts game resumed, interrupted only by the occasional arrival of a press release from the governor's office or one of the departments.

The tempo of the cluttered and scarred old room around the corner from the governor's office was set and enforced by Wes Johns, the dean of the Capitol correspondents. His position was strictly based on his twenty-plus years seniority, but it made him the unchallenged king of the newsies in the pressroom.

The first month I got there, I was watching the game—shorttimers aren't invited to sit in and those whose jib Wes didn't like the cut of weren't called to the table for a year or more—when a handout from the conservation department was dropped off.

It wasn't much—an announcement of dates for hearings on the trout season for the following year, I think, and I took one of the releases off the stack and went over to the *CR&P* desk and began to dial the paper.

"Hold on there, buster!" Wes yelled from the card table. "That ain't how we do it here."

I stopped dialing and looked at Wes, who had slammed his cards down on the table and was standing. "You just come back over here and watch the game for a while," he said.

"But this is an item our sports page will want," I said.

"And it's an item my papers will want for the front page," said Wes, who covered the capital for a string of small dailies in the upstate resort region. "But it ain't something that is gonna stop presses anywhere, and I got a damn good hand here. You just wait till we're done. We don't go for cheap scoops here."

I put down the phone and waited about ten minutes while Wes played out his hand, which I think netted him eighty-five cents. Then he and the other players got up, picked up press releases, and after everyone was seated at their desks, Wes nodded and the fiercely competitive Capitol press corps began to compete.

I noticed that even the wire service reporters conformed to Wes's rules and after the game resumed, I asked Lew Fraser, the young National Press reporter who had about six months seniority on me in the statehouse, how come.

"I thought you guys had 'a deadline every minute,'" I said.

"That's right, but in this place Wes keeps the clock. One time he had a run of hot hands and everybody had to sit on an eighty-million-dollar highway contract announcement for most of an hour."

"Screw that," I said. "If something good comes in, I'm going with it."

"Suit yourself, Bob," Fraser said. "But don't be surprised if your copies of the governor's speech texts or the legislative calendar get lost on the way to the pressroom."

"He can do that?"

"Damn betcha. My bureau chief says when he was here we had to make the rounds twice a day to every department for handouts. Then Wes broke his foot coon hunting and arranged for them all to send their stuff over. He got it and he can stop it."

So I waited like everyone else until Wes was ready to work, and in time—eight months, I think—Wes sauntered over one morning and announced: "Poor Bing Johnson. The state editor of his paper dropped dead yesterday, and he's got to go back there and replace him. You know how to play hearts?"

I did and in fact picked up eight to ten bucks a week regularly from Wes and his buddies until Bing came back, having found the promotion, as he feared, required a full day's work. He got transferred back to the capital after a year by conspiring with Wes to make his replacement miss a couple of good stories and then telling his publisher that they were doomed to be skunked unless he was put back on the state-house beat.

I gave up my seat without protest, and henceforth got along with Wes, who invariably referred to me as "that lucky kid" who "won a couple of hands here."

It was a quiet time at the statehouse and I was able to go by the secretary of state's office to pull out the incorporation papers filed by the *CR&P*'s new owners. Fred Bannerwald, the secretary, was a bigger snoop than any reporter I ever knew, and when I told him what I wanted, got the documents out without making me sign the register for them. Like the boys in the pressroom, Fred also wanted to know what was going on at the paper.

There was nothing on the face of the incorporation papers that looked fishy, but two things struck me immediately as odd. First, the new ownership was represented not only by a Chicago law firm, but by an attorney from our state's major city, who got the reputation during a couple of terms in the legislature as a chore boy for the race track interests that were trying to establish a track in the resort region. I had heard people say he had friends who wore six-hundred-dol-lar suits, three-hundred-dollar shoes, and traveled in big black cars with bulletproof windows, but as far as I could tell, that was just wishful gossip around our sleepy little cap-ital town.

The second thing that seemed strange was the statement of purpose of the corporation, called SNS Associates, a wholly owned subsidiary of *All-American Enterprises*. It said the new company intended to engage in the interstate col-lection, processing and transportation of news and advertis-ing. I checked Morgan's old incorporation papers and they didn't say anything about interstate activities or anything about transportation.

"What the hell can it mean?" I asked Grace at the Next Door one evening after work.

"Damned if I know," Grace answered. "But I did notice that the Mighty Midget [one of his names for Shiu, used only off the *CR&P* premises] gets a lot of aviation trade magazines and even some official-looking stuff from the FAA. That's transportation. Think that means they're going to turn us into an airline?"

"Yeah. Air Poland, probably. You don't know any more about all this than me, and you're sitting right under their noses."

Shep Carley interrupted. "I know something. The hairy one has the hots for sex and crime stories."

"Swift?"

"Yeah. He told me to save all the out-of-town blood and gore and sex crime wire stories we don't use. The short items—quirks and chuckles—too."

"What does he do with them?" I asked.

"Takes them into Fargo's, I mean his office. I looked in yesterday on the way back from the water fountain, and he had them stacked up on the desk and was working on what looked like a page dummy. A tabloid dummy, I think."

"Oh," Carley said to Grace, "and tell him about the measuring."

"Well, that was the first week I came back to work," Grace said. "Shiu and some young guy in a skinny suit went around the newsroom measuring distances. It didn't make much sense and when Doralee Green asked Shiu what was going on, he smiled one of those hundred-watters of his and said, 'The improvements we promised, Miss. The improvements.'"

"Is that all Doralee could get out of him? I've seen her push those two perfect cones of hers up to some guy and have him blubbering in ten seconds. Didn't the Doralee treatment work on Shiu?" I asked.

"Like a charm," Carley said with a laugh. "Shiu reached up and patted her on the boob. She yelped and went back to the society desk like she was shot out of a cannon. I sure wish she'd ask me a question."

I waved at the bartender for another Stroh's. "Me too, but that doesn't tell us diddley about what's going on."

"I think we'll find out soon," Grace said. "Ellie Jones upstairs told me old Tom Swift spends an hour a day with the Mighty Midget and comes out with stacks of papers. Yesterday she said Swift told Shiu as he left, 'Don't worry, I'm ready to start now. You just be sure the stuff is going to arrive on time.'"

"Stuff?" I asked. "Sounds like a cocaine shipment."

Whereupon we all turned our interest back to the beer in front of us and the Formosan tag team wrestling match on the TV screen over us.

The answers to the questions began arriving the following week. Two semi-trailer trucks pulled into the newspaper parking lot and, according to Grace, the toughest-looking bunch of roustabouts this side of *On the Waterfront* began unloading. Shiu and Swift supervised the men and within a few hours the lobby of the newsroom was piled high with containers.

Swift then went to his office and brought out a sheet of paper, thumbtacked it to the staff bulletin board, and without a word vanished into the elevator.

Grace called me (and the rest of the reporters who worked outside the office) and told us we better come by the office before checking out for the day. "I don't know if it's good news or bad, but at least it's news. They're going to put in computers."

We were a backwater operation, but most of us knew something about the widespread switch from typewriters to computer terminals in the news business. Someone asked Fargo before the paper changed hands whether we would be going to VDTs and he replied, "Mr. Morgan says they're gimmicks."

But gimmicks or not, there was what looked like enough cartons and crates to outfit a major polar expedition waiting to be unpacked in the newsroom and a "Memorandum to the Staff" on the bulletin board:

Effective Monday next, the process of producing this newspaper with state-of-the-art electronic word processing and editing equipment will begin.

During the coming weekend, half of the newsroom will be prepared for installation of the new equipment and training the staff for its use. The existing desks will be consolidated within the newsroom and regular daily production of the newspaper will be continued without interruption. The staff is expected to maintain its present high standards of work during the temporary unavoidable crowding that will be caused by the installation of the new equipment.

Training on the new equipment will be conducted by expert technicians engaged by *All-American Enterprises* beginning at 4:00 P.M. Monday. All editorial employees will be present at that time for a one-hour orientation session and to receive their assigned periods to receive "hands-on" instruction in use of the new facilities.

(When she read that, Doralee flounced up to Grace and announced that no ape from Chicago was going to cop a feel from her while pretending to be teaching her how to use a computer. "My boyfriend is six feet six and he's going to be here with me when I get my training," she said.)

The bulletin went on:

Some dramatic and exciting changes will be coming to the *Register & Press* in coming months, of which the installation of the new equipment is only the first. The electronic writing and editing system will permit all involved in the newspaper to increase our productivity and publish a product that will be competitive in an era of high technology.

This change will be made with the utmost regard for the needs and requirements of the *Register & Press* staff. Ample time will be devoted to the instructional process and familiarization with the new equipment. Therefore, the enthusiastic cooperation of every individual on the newspaper staff will be expected. Anything else will be dealt with by disciplinary action, up to and including summary discharge.

S. Shiu, Publisher

"Iron fist under the velvet glove," Bicker said as he stood at the bulletin board with some of us "outside" staffers who had come into the office to look at the boxes and read the bulletin. "Now is when these guys are going to start squeezing us old-timers. They know damn well some of us aren't going to be able to work with these things and it's going to be their chance to toss us out on the street."

"No such thing, old boy," said Swift, who had come up behind the group at the bulletin board. "This system is no harder to use than a typewriter, and anyone who can't cope with it will be assigned alternative duties while they get extra training. We don't want to throw anyone out on the street . . . except, possibly, malcontents."

He stared coldly at Bicker, who, for the first time in anyone's memory, had no argument. "OK, Mr. Swift. I'm going to give it my damndest."

"I'm sure everyone will," Swift said as he turned away.

The next Monday was a national holiday and the statehouse was closed. I went into the office to write a feature and, of course, to see what was happening. All of the desks had been crowded into the front half of the newsroom, but except for a bit of sidling to get from one place to another, work was progressing without too much difficulty. But the three desks that usually were open for use by reporters had been stacked against a wall, so there was no place to work except at one of the news desks. I pulled up a chair at Carley's desk and slid his typewriter around so I could use it while he worked over the wire copy with scissors and copy pencil.

The rear of the newsroom was entirely different. New Formica-topped tables, each with a shiny new computer terminal, had been set up, and half a dozen technicians were busy checking wiring and the computer keyboards and screens. The stained and cigarette-scarred old tile floor had been covered with a light blue rug, and three electricians were on ladders replacing the old hanging bulb fixtures with new fluorescent lights. The place looked like before and after in an office furniture catalogue.

"It's supposed to be ready by four this afternoon, but I doubt it," Shep muttered as he worked over the wire copy. "I heard when they went to wire the new lights and put power in for the computers, they found the existing wiring had been installed about 1910 and had been pulled through illuminating gas conduits. We're probably lucky we weren't burned out of here years ago."

The techs were still fiddling with the machines at the appointed hour, but Shiu, Swift, and one of the best-looking females I had seen in months appeared in the newsroom on the tick of the hour. The staff, afraid to set foot in the renovated part of the room, perched on the old desks.

"Now then," Shiu began. "We'll just ask the installation people to take a break for thirty minutes and the staff please will gather around for a brief talk. Thank you."

Shiu waited while the sixteen of us moved into the new section and settled into the molded plastic chairs that had been set out at the desks.

"What you see around you here is the newsroom of a modern newspaper, or it will be when the project is completed," Shiu said. "*All-American Enterprises* has spared no expense in providing the staff of this newspaper with the latest, state-of-the-art equipment. It will be several weeks before we are in a position actually to produce the newspaper with this equipment, but I promise you we will do it.

"*The Capital Register & Press* is a fine and proud newspaper, but it is woefully behind the times, in facilities as well as news concepts. This is the beginning of a new day for the *CR&P*. Now, I would like you to meet Miss Gail Overstreet, who will be the leader of the tutorial group that will instruct all of you in the use of our fine new computers. Miss Overstreet."

The lady, tall and lithe with long dark hair worn in the style of the knockout woman lawyer on "Hill Street Blues," stepped up next to Shiu, whose head barely reached her bosom.

"Are you afraid?" she asked, pausing dramatically. "Afraid of these machines? Don't answer—I've been through these scenes a dozen times and I know that many of you are—except for those of you who have computers at home. Anybody?"

Farley Free, the second sports man, and Mo Gealber, the business writer, raised their hands, both looking sheepishly around as if they had just admitted peeking into a girls' locker room.

"Excellent. You two gentlemen will be of value to me and my two associates in the coming weeks. But let me caution you all. These machines are not your simple fun-in-the-living-room toys. What you see here are powerful terminals which are the simplest peripherals of a rather sophisticated main frame computer being installed in a room on the first floor of this building. They are not toys. They are the tools that will permit you to produce a newspaper faster and better than any of you had dreamed possible.

"Mr. Shiu said that this is a modern newsroom. Ladies and gentlemen, it is one step beyond that. It is the media production environment of the next century. You are the last of your profession who will use such antiquated implements as pencils and pens and scissors and paste to publish a newspaper. You are the last who will have to wrestle with paper to put out a paper."

She spread her arms wide and smiled like she had just

discovered a cure for the common cold: "Welcome, my friends, to the electronic newsroom!"

Most of us looked at one another as if this broad had just announced that we were about to board a spaceship for Mars. But Shiu and Swift began applauding, joined by Fargo, the eternal company man, and then by about half of the staff. They didn't know why the hell they were clapping, but they dutifully beat their palms just the same in case it was something important.

(A week later, after I had managed to get into the Overstreet underwear, I asked what had been the purpose of that speech inasmuch as the staff had no choice about using the new machines. "The opening remarks are for the management," she said. "It makes them feel smart, having plunked down all that dough for a bunch of machines they don't know the first thing about and probably will never learn to use. But the rest was for you working stiffs.")

And the rest of the speech was just that. Dick Mooniman, our police reporter, said the last time he heard something like that was his first day at Parris Island—back when the Marine drill instructors didn't have to worry about some momma's boy writing his congressman to complain he had been made to march in a swamp with real snakes.

What the lovely Miss Overstreet told us, in brief, was that (1) we would have a reasonable time to learn to use the computers, (2) two weeks of two-hour-a-day after-work training was a reasonable time, and (3) anyone who couldn't cut it in that time either was too slow to ever work in the "electronic newsroom" or was doping off. Either way, the message came clear, it was swim or sink in two weeks.

After that, the lady read off a list of names assigned to her and two other instructors. I was on her list along with Cindy Korth, my statehouse backup, Judy Teach, the city hall reporter, Mooniman, Bill Grace, and Shep Carley.

The training started that afternoon. She was good at it and patient with those of us who had just barely mastered the manual typewriter before the computer and Gail Overstreet came into our lives.

I, of course, fell in love with the teacher. Maybe it was that long and thick black hair, or maybe the challenge of breaking through that steel-edged control she maintained on the job. It took about four days and a couple pitchers of martinis to get behind that facade and discover that she was just as tough as met the eye, but also just as lonesome as any traveling salesman gets on the road.

I was fascinated; this was a new kind of woman to me. I had married young because it had seemed the thing to do in those days and found myself alternately bored and angered by the constraints of nesting. So I strayed early and often, looking for something I couldn't describe and never really found. Most of what I discovered was a variety of sex and what it got me was a divorce.

All of us learned how to use that computer in the allotted two weeks and, with the benefit of some very private "hands on" tutoring from Gail, I learned some other things about the system that were to be valuable.

Gail gave each of us a "password" that was supposed to safeguard our notes and other confidential material we might otherwise store in locked file cabinets or shoeboxes in the back of a closet. Later, she told me what anyone with any logical sense would have realized—that the passwords were stored in a directory in the computer so it could recognize legitimate users. Anyone who knew how to decode the passwords would be able to read anything in the system. Later than that, just before the two weeks and our brief romp ended with Gail's departure for another assignment, she told me how to find that directory. There was a price, but it was a relatively palatable one.

I used what Gail told me and an offhand remark by a colleague not long after that to discover what Shiu and Swift were up to.

CHAPTER 3

Ordinarily, I had a drink or two after work at the bar in the Clark Hotel, where in season you usually could find a member of the legislature and almost always a lobbyist or two eager to pop for a jar in return for an ear or an answer.

On that last, my conscience was clear: I never gave a lobbyist information that I had not first used in a story. But somehow, they seemed to think they were getting a better brand of news over a $1.75 martini than they could from a two-bit paper. The way I looked at it, when the paper started paying wages that could support my modest thirst, I would be more selective in my drinking companions—and even buy once in a while myself. Meantime, the lobbyists were contributing to the upkeep of a free and independent press by buying their news twice.

During the computer training period, I spent a lot more time than usual in the office, and after the sessions, when I wasn't pursuing the teacher, at the Next Door with Grace, Carley, and people like Drew Claggett, Judy Teach, and Farley Free, all of whom had a lively sense of gossip and no need to rush home after work.

Before Shiu and Swift arrived, the talk at the bar was mostly sports and gossip about who was trying to get whom into bed. I didn't care that much about sports and I was more interested in making gossip than listening to it, so the Next Door usually didn't hold that much attraction to me. But with the arrival of the new management, Topic A was the paper and what was going to happen to it and us.

The first hint came about a week after the computers arrived. I had struck out trying to date Gail Overstreet and was seeking solace and company in the booth usually occupied by *CR&P* staffers. We were talking about an item that had run on page two of that day's edition. It had a one-column headline in relatively modest type:

THIEVES GET
TRIBE'S GOAT

MAZUNDI, Zardia (NP)—Gratou tribal chief Rawindi Azabandi recently passed a sentence of death on two tribesmen who were caught milking a ritual goat, travelers returning to this capital from the interior reported.

The men were cooked and eaten at the tribe's annual spring reunion at the 38,000-seat soccer stadium recently built for the Gratous by Albanian technicians. Mazundi defeated a visiting team from Rampistan following the ceremony, 3–2.

When I saw that, I knew something radical was happening at the paper. Before I got the statehouse beat, I had worked in Carley's job, and I remembered well Fargo's instructions for handling wire service stories.

"No freaks, no geeks," he had said. "No cannibalism. No weird sex murders. Mr. Morgan publishes a family newspaper. He doesn't want phone calls from ministers and little old ladies. Especially Mrs. Morgan's friends."

Carley, as usual, had been one of the first to arrive at the bar, and he had already explained the story's presence in the paper to a succession of staffers. By the time I arrived, Carley had a good start on the night's drinking and was somewhat defensive.

"Don't blame me. I know the paper's policy and I told Swift when he gave me the item. But he just said, 'Bugger the policy. I'm the M.E. now and I say run it.'"

Claggett was the member of the group who had the widest

experience. He had worked on papers in Minneapolis, Sioux City, and Chicago, including a couple that had gone belly up. But he was an accomplished editor and rewrite man, and like the fast short-order cook, the honest bartender, and the clever auto mechanic, he could get a job just about any place he decided to get off the bus. On matters dealing with the real world of newspapering, he was the arbiter.

"This wouldn't be a big thing in practically any other town," he said. "Hell, small town papers all over the place are spicing up the product, and this item really ain't much to get excited about. I remember the time the Sioux City paper ran an AP photo of Siamese twins joined at the head. The editor spent a month going around to women's clubs apologizing. But it sure comes as a shock to see something like this in a dull old rag like the *CR&P*."

"Well, I think there's going to be more of it," Carley said. "Swift has been reading every story on the diet doctor murder trial, and he asked me today if there had been any follow-up to a piece we ran last week about a photographer's model being mauled by a lion during a picture-taking session for a tire commercial."

"Here's something else that fits in with what Shep was talking about," Judy Teach said. "I got a memo from Swift this week asking if there had been any charges of sexual harrassment of female employes at city hall," and when I told him yesterday that there hadn't, he said, 'Pity.' At least that's what I think he said."

Carley was so right. The next day there was an item on the sports page about a zookeeper who had one of his gorillas trained to forecast football games by picking slips of paper with team names written on them out of his hand. That headline, over a picture of the gorilla, was:

APE MAKES MONKEYS
OF SPORTS PUNDITS

That night at the bar, Free was cooking mad about the story. He said Swift had come over to the sports desk with the story and the photo and instructed Hank Terry to run it at the top of the page.

"That son of a bitch," Free said. "When Terry told him after reading the story that the gorilla had a better forecasting record than we did, he said, 'All the better, old boy. Nothing like the local angle to pull the reader in, what?' Then as he was walking away, he said, 'See if you can find out if the zoo in this town has a gorilla.'"

"Does it?" Claggett asked.

"Yeah," said Free. "But all he can do is read copy and write headlines."

The gorilla story wasn't the only piece Swift had ordered into the paper that day. On the third page, there was a wire story from Missouri about a girlie magazine owner who was found in contempt of court for venting his feelings when he was brought before a judge and charged with distributing obscene matter.

Carley said the wire service editors had quoted the accused but had run a discretionary slug on the story, calling editors' attention to the nature of the copy.

We usually passed up stories like that unless they were of local interest, and we always used dots or asterisks in the place of profanity. But at Swift's order, there were the pornographer's very words in the stodgy old *CR&P*: "shithead," "asshole," and "piss on you."

The two-column headline, written by Swift, read:

PORN CZAR IN SLAMS
FOR CUSSING JUDGE

But the prize Swift headline for that day was on the front page—over a story about dissident members of the Palestine Liberation Front defying their long-time leader:

ARABS WON'T
SAY YASSER

There was another Swift special a few pages back—a story about a movement on Staten Island to secede from New York City. The headline was:

STATEN ISLE TO
N.Y.—BYE BYE

"Swift explained that one to me when he brought it out," Carley said. "He said it was a send-up, whatever the hell that is."

"Sure," Claggett said. "Like a spoof. He was talking about the famous *Daily News* headline when Jerry Ford opposed the federal bailout of the city—'Ford to New York: Drop Dead.'"

The subject seemingly exhausted, the conversation turned to the other big issue in our working lives—learning to use the computer.

That day, Gail and her two associates had explained the password system for storing our files and had told each of us to select a word of up to eight characters to use as our personal "keys" into the computer's memory.

"The trick," Free, the computer buff, said, "is to choose a password that you will easily remember, but isn't your name or initials, so everybody won't go poking around in your files. I don't plan to file anything really confidential. I think I'll use an easy play on my name—'NOCHARGE.'"

"I like it," Grace said. "I'll use 'PRAYER.'"

"That's great," I said, "but what the hell am I going to use? What would be a play on the name 'Wartovsky'?"

"PIMPLE," Shep Carley offered.

"Thanks a lot," I said. "And why don't you use 'DOG' for 'Shepard'?"

"Well, you don't have to do it that way," Free said. "You can choose any combination of eight letters or numbers. If you don't care about keeping your password secret, you can even use your first or last name."

"By the way," Grace said, "Shiu told me today that they will be putting computer terminals in the beat reporters' pressrooms. You'll get one at city hall, Judy, and Bob will have one at the Capitol. Those will have locks so people don't fool around with them when you're not there."

Sure enough, a couple of days later, a technician showed up at the pressroom with a computer terminal. It took him about an hour to install the machine, and when he left, the card players gathered around while I showed off my new gadget.

Wes pronounced the machine useless. "Damn thing looks too delicate for me," he said. "I like a typewriter I can pound and give a kick once in a while. And where the hell are you if a fuse blows right in the middle of writing a story? At least with a typewriter, you don't lose everything you've written."

"Besides," Wes said with a leer, "I hear these things will fry your *cojones*. Doesn't that bother you, kid?"

Like the instant expert I was, I explained to Wes that copy could be stored in the computer memory as you went along; even if the power went off you could retrieve it later. And the radiation I said, with a show of confidence not altogether felt, wasn't any worse than you would get sitting close to a color television set.

"I was talking about sittin' close to a woman," Wes said, returning to the hearts game.

The arrival of my own computer reminded me that I had not yet chosen a password, and Gail was pushing all of us to have them that afternoon.

I had an idea of what I wanted to use (ROBOT, a play on my formal given name), but thought I'd use my extra training to look at what the others had selected first. I used the method she had explained the previous night to call up the directory of passwords on the screen.

Most of the staff had made their choices. Free's

NOCHARGE and Grace's PRAYER were there, and I guessed at some of the others—LUNAR, I figured was Dick Mooniman; Hank Terry had selected his newsroom nickname, SNICKER; Darlington had chosen his first name, SAM; and Doralee Green, ever flaunting her cultural background, obviously was the VERDI in the directory. It wasn't until she told me later that I could figure out why Cindy had chosen CAPTWO (Number 2 at the capitol), and I was also stopped temporarily, by BIRD.

That one came to me when I recalled Farley's suggestion for choosing an easily remembered name. A Swift was a BIRD, and I had found the managing editor's password. What was there to do but take a look at what the hairy one had filed away?

The first couple of items were memos to the staff, which I had read on the city room bulletin board. But the last item was something else—a private memo from Swift to Shiu.

"Update of *Capital Register & Press* Editorial Plan," it read. It went on to report that the installation of the computers and the new furniture in the newsroom had been completed and that satisfactory progress had been made in training the staff to use the computers. It continued as follows:

Project A.M. Tabloid is proceeding according to the timetable for the editorial staff. The process of gradual introduction into the paper of editorial material suitable to the plan is proceeding without significant resistance.

Note: The switchboard reported eight telephoned protests to the African story and twenty-two on the pornography item. Barton received six letters protesting the first story and seventeen on the second, including a boycott threat from one women's garden group. I am informed that there has been some grumbling about the items in and around the newsroom, but this can be discounted as the usual griping to be heard from newspaper staffs.

In all, our first efforts to inject some color and life into the newspaper have encountered somewhat less resistance than we anticipated, and it now appears that your proposal to accelerate the elements of the plan can be carried out. It is assumed that you will contact our principals for approval of the amended timetable.

While the following is wholly within your jurisdiction as publisher, I feel it should be pointed out that if acceleration is approved, it will be necessary to begin immediately the conversion of physical facilities in the production department as well as arrange for earlier-than-planned acquisition of the transport equipment. Considering the amount of lead time required for the latter, I suggest that you make entirely certain that you will be able to meet an accelerated timetable. Our principals, as you well know, do not take slippages lightly.

The memo was dated three days before I found it, and Shiu obviously had moved quickly. As I walked up the alley beside the paper on the way to the last computer training session that afternoon, I ran into Willy Janzen, the composing room foreman.

"Hey, you ready to be a tabloid reporter? The Jap just told us to start adjusting for tab size next week. You gonna have to write those whore's dreams of yours a lot shorter now, Bobby."

The tabloid word had already spread inside the newsroom when I got there, but it appeared no one had been told yet that the *CR&P* was going to become a morning newspaper as well. I was just whispering that bit of news to Grace when he got a call to come up to Shiu's office. He was back in ten minutes with confirmation: "Week after next, we go A.M. We got one week to get used to the tabloid size and then we go to morning publication. Swift has the work schedules all made up."

All of that was so much to assimilate I forgot to tell Grace about the reference to "transport equipment." That was to be our next big surprise. It was to be later, much later, before we found out about the "principals" Swift mentioned in his memo.

CHAPTER 4

I got my biggest story because somebody parked in my space at the Capitol. Actually, I got two stories from that circumstance, but the first was maybe the dumbest story I ever covered on the statehouse beat.

When I found a blue Honda parked in the space reserved for my green Plymouth, I did what any self-respecting scrounger would—I parked in someone else's space. But later in the day, it occurred to me that the blue Honda now had succeeded in screwing up two people, and that was sufficient motivation to take a trip to the Capitol police office in the basement.

When I got to the office the 4:00 P.M. to midnight shift was just coming to work. I asked the secretary to see the chief and she waved me to a seat.

"He's got someone with him, Bob. Shouldn't be long."

It wasn't long, but it sure was loud. Chief Jimmy McGrath was chewing ass, and the decibel level was high enough to peel paint off a wall.

"Don't tell me it didn't happen on your watch, goddamn it! It was there this morning and there wasn't anyone in the goddamn building after your shift went off at midnight," McGrath yelled. "It had to be on your shift."

A quieter voice: "But Jimmy . . ."

"Don't Jimmy me, you fucking lunkhead. Just because you're my wife's nephew don't give you privileges here. It's chief, and I wish to God it had been you with the title this morning when the governor called me up there. You know how mad a man can get when he finds turd on his one-hundred-and-twenty-dollar Eyetalian shoes? Madder than I am at you and if I get any madder I'm liable to make you the only police lieutenant in the state to be assigned as a crossing guard. Now get your ass out of here."

The lieutenant, a ratty little guy named Orris, was out of McGrath's office before the echo had died, and the secretary smiled at me and said, "He can see you now, Bob."

I knew I wasn't supposed to have heard what had been said before my arrival, so I confined my conversation with the chief to the parking problem.

"It don't help for you to park in somebody else's spot, Bob," said McGrath, still red around the jowls but trying to be pleasant. "Tell you what. If this happens again, drive over to the Capitol and park by the basement entrance and come on down here to get me or an officer. We'll just start towing anybody's ass out of that lot if they don't have a sticker."

That seemed to end our business, but I sure did want to know what Orris had done to earn the chewing he got. So I tried the old I-know-what's-going-on gambit.

"Boy, chief, you sure were right about the governor. He was in a crappy mood—excuse the pun—all day."

McGrath went for it: "I'd have been too . . . stepping into a pile of shit right in the middle of the Capitol rotunda. If somebody thinks that's a joke, about six months in the can ought to change his mind. It wasn't the first time, either."

"You mean we've got a rash of dumpings in the Capitol?"

"Twice before, somebody found . . . hey, you ain't going to write about this, are you?"

"Desecration of public property, chief. But don't worry, I won't make a big thing out of it. Just an item in my column and I'll use the angle that you have a lead on the perpetrator. I know damn well Orris is going to try to catch the guy after the chewing you gave him."

I left the chief's office and hunted down Orris. On him, I used the old cop trick—sympathy.

"Seems to me Jimmy was kind of tough on you, lieutenant. After all, the building is unpatrolled from when you leave at midnight till the morning shift comes on."

"Yeah, but he's right that there's nobody here after we lock up," Orris said. An odd look passed over his face. "Nobody but the goddamn night watchman and his goddamn dog . . . his goddamn dog, goddamn it." Orris headed toward the Capitol basement at a run.

I went on to the pressroom and, after checking with McGrath to make sure the culprit had been identified, tapped out a kicker for my regular weekly statehouse tidbits column:

CASE CLOSED—Capitol police last week solved a nasty little mystery that has been causing high-level consternation for several months. Someone or something had been leaving deposits on the marble floors of the Capitol in the middle of the night. It turned out to be the night watchman's Doberman, who from now on will be walked outdoors before he goes on patrol with the watchman each night.

Cute, I thought—until the phone rang and Swift asked, "How long has that animal been shitting on our Capitol floors?"

I made the mistake of being flattered that Swift had noticed the item. "Oh, two or three months. The cops didn't really get excited about it until today when the governor stepped in it."

"The governor stepped in it? What did he say?"

"Well, I don't really know. I know he was mad as hell. . . ."

"Wartovsky, I thought you were one of the few actual

reporters on this benighted newspaper. Find out what the governor said. Call him and ask him. Get a quote, you idiot!"

Without thinking what Swift had in mind, I called the governor's office. It was past five, so it was no surprise that he wasn't in. When I phoned Swift, it sounded as if he had calmed down. He said, in a tight, cold tone, "If there is no way to reach him tonight, I suppose we'll have to make do. But I want you to follow up on this. Get a comment tomorrow."

My surprise came the next morning. Just below the fold on the front page was a two-column headline:

PHANTOM OF ROTUNDA NABBED BY COPS AT STATE CAPITOL

By ROBERT WARTOVSKY
Register Press Capitol Correspondent

The phantom of the Capitol rotunda, a midnight desecrator who left his "calling card" on the pristine marble floors of the state's most hallowed building, has been apprehended and is being rehabilitated, police reported late yesterday.

Capitol sources revealed that the perpetrator was guilty of at least three despoilations of the building in the past few months, but until yesterday Chief James McGrath's police force, composed principally of patronage appointees, had no clue to his identity or his modus operandi.

It was known, however, that the phantom operated only after midnight when the regular police force turns Capitol security over to a (patronage) night watchman, but neither the late-shift police patrol nor the watchman purported to have any idea how or when the dirty deposits were being left in the building.

It was only yesterday morning when Governor Schmid stepped into the most recent desecration of the floor in the rotunda that Chief McGrath and his minions (who are paid thirty-two percent more than city police) felt impelled to give the investigation of the incidents higher priority.

"The governor really fried Jimmy McGrath's behind, and he passed the same treatment on to his underlings," a Capitol source said last night.

Police Lt. Guy Orris, commanding the 4:00 P.M. to midnight shift at the Capitol, made the arrest after receiving a severe tongue-lashing from Chief McGrath, reliable sources said.

Orris, who had no known investigative experience before his appointment, but was involved in the Schmid campaign in the last election, discovered the offender after being aided by the *Capital Register & Press* Capitol correspondent in winnowing the potential suspects.

The culprit was identified as Donnerwenter, a five-year-old Doberman pinscher owned by Augustus Fingo, the Capitol night watchman. Fingo was understood to be a distant relative of Secretary of State Fred Bannerman.

Sources said that henceforth Donnerwenter would be walked outdoors each night before accompanying Fingo on his postmidnight rounds. The case was closed with red faces all around.

I was flat-out panicked when I read the piece. Who could have done such a thing? Could I go to the Capitol today? Or ever? I leaped for the phone and dialed the paper, intending to reach Grace and fry his ears with my objections to what had been done to my story.

I forgot that none of the regular staff would be on duty at 9 A.M. now that the paper had switched to morning publication. Diana Osky, the feature writer, answered, and frightened by my shouting, switched me to the only news executive on hand—Swift.

"What seems to be the problem, old man?" Swift asked.

"My story!" I yelled. "Somebody took that little item about the dog crapping in the Capitol and turned it into a major production! And it's full of stuff I never had in my story."

Swift's voice took on the cold tone of the previous night. "Yes, it is fleshed out somewhat. You barely had enough information in what you reported to sustain a story for the front page. However, we were able to make do with a little research and a few telephone calls."

"Who's responsible for this? I won't be able to show my face in the Capitol."

The voice went from cold to glacial. "The story was written by Mr. Wilks under my supervision, Mr. Wartovsky. If you have complaints, address them to me.

"And as for not showing your face at the Capitol, I would suggest you get off your bum and out of that pressroom and bring us some printable news for a change. There ought to be four or five good human interest yarns a day around that building and up to now, the only story I've seen from you that approached adequacy was the dog piece . . . and you all but buried that. A good reporter would have interviewed the night watchman—you can be bloody well sure the network telly people already have—and, for God's sake, you didn't even think to call the photographer to bring us a shot of the dog, and the place in the rotunda he fouled.

"A rum piece of work, Mr. Wartovsky. You can start today to recover from it by doing a follow-up on the dog story . . . and I want it to have something from the governor." Swift slammed the phone down.

Scared? I hadn't popped sweat like that since my first week on a small town paper upstate when the high school football coach got killed in an auto accident. The word came in while I was in the office alone, and I couldn't even remember the guy's first name and didn't have a clue on how to even start getting a story together. It came to me that the easy days were over at the *Register & Press*, and I was entering the new era with my name at the top of the management's shit list.

I got dressed and drove to the Capitol, where I got lucky and didn't run into either Orris or McGrath. Joe Mosser, the cop who was stationed at the parking lot (and often was somewhere else drinking coffee or propositioning clerk-typists), was on duty when I pulled in. As I stopped at his guard shack, he grinned and said, "Oh, welcome, Mr. Wartovsky. Your parking place awaits, Mr. Wartovsky. You will be interested to know, Mr. Wartovsky, that your bitch about the parking got me a royal chewing out. But that was before he saw your story this morning. From what I've heard on the radio today, you better not so much as drop a cigarette butt in the Capitol. In fact, don't drop one in the parking lot, either. Littering the Capitol grounds is a fifty-dollar rap, pal."

In the pressroom, the card players paused when I came in but went back to their game without the usual hellos. Lew Fraser came up wearing a worried look and perched on my desk.

"Wes says you're cut off from any goodies he has anything to say about. Says anybody who stoops to a cheap needle job to make front page isn't worthy of the fellowship of serious Capitol reporters."

Fraser grinned. "It was quite a hype, but a hell of a piece. We took out the political references and got it on the national wire this morning. And the Chicago desk didn't even try to jazz it up."

I was numb. "OK, Lew, to hell with Wes. I didn't write the piece that way, but I'm damned if I'll explain that to him or any other of those hacks. Let me tell you something—I think we're going to see stuff in my paper from now on that will make that story look like a Sunday school exercise. The new M.E. is starting to take control and it looks like it's going to get weird."

I dialed the governor's press secretary, Phil Goldberg. His secretary told me in a very small voice that she'd see if he was in.

"You shmuck!" (He was in) "You bastard. Haven't we always played ball with you? What kind of cheap shot was that? Are you just trying to make this administration look stupid? The governor's so pissed he gave up his golf game after nine holes this morning."

"Can I talk to him? To explain."

"Nega-tive, kiddo. He says he ain't saying anything to anyone from the Daily Crap-ola today or maybe forever."

"The piece didn't knock him."

"No, but it made his Capitol cops look like the Keystone brigade and so far he's concerned, that's a crack at him. Jimmy McGrath and the governor have been through some thick together, and I'm surprised you didn't know that."

"Well, I can explain what happened if I can talk to him. I'll only need five minutes, tops."

"Sorry, he's not in."

"Come on, Phil. Not in to me or really not in?"

"Not in. Really. Out of town. But even if he was, I doubt he would be to you for a couple of days."

For some reason, probably because I thought it would serve him right for hyping my story, I phoned Swift to tell him that the governor was not talking to the *Register & Press* now or for the foreseeable future. Besides, he was out of town.

Surprisingly, Swift took it well. "So that's his game, eh? Well, we have more than one arrow in our quiver, old boy. For today, that will be all we'll require. But I want you to call Schmid's office every morning until further notice, and I want you to begin keeping a log of his absences from the Capitol. I'll notify you later what we will do with that information."

I found out—from Lew Fraser—that Swift didn't give up that easily. He called the National Press Bureau and, as a client, requested National Press to seek a comment from the governor on the dog story. Lew, of course, had the request bucked to him, and got the same reply minus the vituperation from Goldberg. The governor was out of town. He didn't say where.

Given that answer, Swift called the bureau chief at Amalgamated News, who had come sniffing around the *Capital Register & Press* after the change of ownership hoping to sell his service. Swift told that worthy that his competition had failed on a request and asked him if AN would like to show what it could do. So Park Withers, Fraser's competition, got to try Goldberg. He had the presence of mind to ask where the governor was. Upstate was the answer.

All of this produced an unusual amount of traffic on the service wires of both NP and AN, and several wire editors around the state noticed it and got curious enough to phone their Capitol reporters. So it was that Wes Johns was pulled, protesting, from his hearts game, to the telephone. I could hear him protesting that it was strictly a *Cap & Reg* furor, but agreeing after more argument to try to get a comment from the governor. Goldberg was scared of Wes and told him the governor was out of town, visiting Oakdale to inspect some soil conservation work, but he would call there and ask the governor to contact Wes as soon as possible.

Two hours later, Wes got a call from Oakdale and a no comment from the governor.

The next day, after being reminded by Grace that Swift still wanted a follow-up from the governor on the dog story, I called Goldberg again. "He's still not in, Bob. He went from Oakdale to West Adams last night, and he'll be touring daycare facilities all day."

"Did you give him my request for a comment on that story?"

"Sure. He said to tell you to ask Wes Johns for his comment."

"You mean the no comment he gave Wes?"

"No, something special he gave Wes for you."

I asked Wes.

The dean of Capitol correspondents looked over his half-glasses and announced, "I'm a deacon of my church, Wartovsky. I won't repeat what he told me to tell you. But I can tell you it had something to do with you having sexual congress with a web-footed waterfowl."

The next day, I called Goldberg and got yet another dodge.

"Just missed him, Bob. He was in town overnight—came by the Capitol early this morning and was off to the city for the rest of the week. He's got appointments with bankers on the state bond issues, and he's going to look in on a couple of juvenile halfway houses. I know he'll be in Chicago during the weekend, but I don't know the schedule for next week."

"Phil, this sounds like a runaround. Is he really doing this much traveling or are you diddling me?"

"Swear to God, Bob, he's on the road. With the legislature out, he figures he can get out and around and listen to people and see what is happening away from this town. He figures nobody here tells him the truth about what is going on in the state."

"Can you get me the schedule for next week before the weekend?"

"I'll try, but if it's like this week, he's been making it up on the fly. You know, it's his chance to be a little less schedule-driven. But I'll try."

The whole thing sounded odd to me, and when I told Swift about it, he was even more skeptical.

"Tell me, does this fellow normally spend a lot of time away from the capital?"

"No," I said. "In his first term he hardly left town at all, and he's done very little traveling since he started his second. If he wasn't already serving the last term he's allowed or if a Senate seat was coming vacant next year, I'd guess he was lining up the ducks for a campaign. And the places he went this week don't make any political sense. It's like he picked them out of a hat."

The partial schedule Goldberg produced late that week was even more mysterious. Monday and part of Tuesday in the state's biggest city visiting social service centers for the elderly and Wednesday and Thursday in the medium-sized towns of Morrow, Severs, and Manville checking out water treatment facilities and a state highway bridge project. Friday, he was scheduled to conduct pardon hearings in Watertown at the state penitentiary.

These all were certainly plausible and proper activities for any governor, but Schmid was making this round of the state without any press hoopla—even in the towns he was visiting. Goldberg said the media of course was welcome to cover his activities, but we would have to handle our own travel and lodging arrangements because the governor's office was making no provisions for a press contingent to accompany him. Odd, odd, odd.

Swift, who by this time had apparently forgiven me, or forgotten that he was mad at me, appeared fascinated by my report on the latest word from Goldberg.

"I agree with you, Bob. This is entirely uncharacteristic of the governor in light of what you have told me. I want you and Tandee to pick him up Monday in the city and tag along all week. Just look and listen and maybe you'll run across something. And if nothing else, you'll come back with a feature on the governor meets his subjects . . . uh, the voters.

"I'll call Mr. Shiu and arrange for you to get expense advances later today. I think he'll go for it on the basis of a demonstration that we are a statewide paper that doesn't just cover the capital.

"One more thing, Bob. I don't want you just to follow him around and take notes on what he says and does. Stay behind at some of these stops and get the reactions of the people. Let's get some names and good quotes . . . and for God's sake, some pictures."

So it was that Whine and I saddled up the company's wheezy Pinto Sunday night and set out for the city, where we were to attach ourselves to the Honorable A. Pinckney Schmid for the next five days. It turned out to be a real trip.

CHAPTER 5

Ah, the city by the lake, the Big Town. I always liked the place because it made no bones about its mission in life—rake in the money and spend it on things you enjoy—like lots of beer and heaping portions of heavy food. To hell with being skinny; eat, drink, and belch happily.

Two examples that tell a lot about the place: The first is what happened to the best relief pitcher in baseball the year the city got a major league team. This fellow had the misfortune to be of the same ethnic persuasion as the majority of the city's population, and by the time they got through stuffing him with sausage chased with beer at testimonial dinners and booster club picnics, he had put on forty pounds and couldn't strike out the batboy, let alone bend over to tie his shoelaces.

Without an effective short reliever that first year, the team finished the same number of games back of first place as its gluttonous pitching ace had gained pounds. Naturally, the front office fired the manager.

It wasn't until the next spring that the team sent the pitcher down to Oshkosh, where he was told to lose what by now had become sixty-five pounds more than his playing weight. Opposing teams had taken to bunting directly at him, and his belly stuck out so far that he lost sight of the ball after it had rolled halfway to the pitcher's mound.

He gave a halfhearted try at dieting, surrendered after a month, and came back to the city where he opened a bar near the stadium. He did so well he now owns a sky box overlooking first base, where he serves miles of wurst and rivers of beer to his friends, who come to listen to him spin oldtimer yarns and even watch a little baseball.

The second example illustrates the city's old world thrift. In this town nothing is thrown away. Faced with a booming population that was generating more sewage than its facilities could handle, the town fathers found a method of transforming the output of the city's toilets into garden fertilizer and marketed it all over the country. They say it's great for tomatoes. The revenues don't exactly finance the school system, but they go a long way toward paying the Sanitation Department's overhead.

Rip Tandee and I got to the city Sunday night, checked into an elegantly faded old hotel that was in its prime when Warren Harding was in his, and headed out for one of those bounteous European dinners that sit in your belly like a rockslide for two or three days after they are eaten. A couple of them and it is easy to see why this is the town that sells most of the size fifty belts in the country.

Bloat notwithstanding, Tandee and I were at the Kleinschiller Golden Age Club at 8:30 the next morning, waiting for the Honorable Schmid.

The old folks, tickled that they were getting so much attention, pressed strudel, bundt cake, and assorted other high-calorie goodies on us, and set up a great buzz about who was going to see his or her picture in the paper tomorrow. They lost some interest when they realized that we were from the paper in the capital, not the city, but Whine, for once, was happy as he snapped away at the old folks.

"Character studies," he chortled as he clicked away. "Contest judges love these old buzzards."

The governor arrived nearly on time and waded into the crowd of oldsters like a rabbit in a cabbage patch. Whine and I tried to get close to hear what was being said and to take pictures, but the old parties were mobbing His Excellency with such fervor that anyone not equipped with a cane or a walker was likely to fetch some mean bruises. Whine complained that one of the old ladies had elbowed him in the stomach: "Jeez, she looked like my grandma but she checked me like a hockey player."

The governor was distinctly not happy to see us, and he grinned like a banshee when the geriatric set surrounded him so thoroughly that we couldn't do anything but back off and stand along a wall while he worked the crowd.

Goldberg wasn't with him. Instead, he had a bulky sergeant from the state troopers running interference for him, and it was touching to watch him try to open a path for Schmid without crushing any elderly voters. Finally he got the governor to a raised platform, where Schmid stepped behind a table and raised his hand.

"I am so happy to be here," he said. "If I had known I would get this kind of reception, I'd have come every time the darn old legislature did something I didn't want. This is a perfectly marvelous boost for an old politician's ego.

"But I'm here for more than shaking hands—I mention that for the benefit of those two press fellows back there, but also because I want to see how this center is serving you, and even more importantly, I want to visit with some of you privately. So if you folks will let us, I'd like to tour the fine facility here and then borrow the center director's office for some powwows with a few of you. I believe our fine director selected five or six people and asked if you would give your governor a little time. Did you get those invitations?"

About half a dozen old folks raised their hands, and the governor acknowledged them with a wave. Then, with the center director leading, he did a quick walk-through, kitchen to card room, and vanished into the director's office.

The six selected oldsters were seated outside, but the big cop, who was known around the Capitol as "Moose" Morse, told us there would be no interviews, before or after, because the governor wanted no pressure on the old folks. So

Whine shot some pictures, and we went back into the main room of the center to talk to the others.

We hung around for about an hour, but the governor didn't reappear and the old folks he talked to apparently were whisked out the back door and taken home because we didn't see them either. Figuring we could corral Schmid for comment on his talks at the next stop, which was after lunch, Whine and I returned to the hotel to have our mid-day meal—ah, that wurst and draft beer—and replenish his film supply. Whine, of course, complained that he didn't have the right cameras for the job, and how come I didn't tell him we'd be working close up in crowds.

The second stop, at a suburban church, went much the same as the first, except the people obviously were a cut richer than the folks at the inner city center and considerably less effusive in their greetings to the governor.

This time, we could follow him as he walked along among the lunch tables, shaking hands, but once again we were shut out when he closeted himself one on one with the oldsters. Before he went into the office, however, he stopped for a second to tell me, "Really, Bob, there's no story here. I'm just talking to these people in private because I think they will be a little more open with me than in some kind of open forum.

"Besides," he said with a wicked grin, "there's no dog doing dirt in any of these places. All of the people so far have had nothing but good to say about the centers."

So we went back to the hotel with more pictures—a lot of quotes from people who didn't talk to the governor—and appetites for another of those Deutschland Über Arteries dinners.

That evening we went by Timmie's, the local newspaper bar. I didn't see anyone I knew, but Whine ran into a photographer acquaintance, and we sat down to trade some lies. Whine bragged that he had taken some potentially prize-winning pictures at the old folks' centers we visited and the local shooter, Jim Raus, got considerably upset at the thought of a small-town visitor coming onto his turf to make hay.

"Shit, we didn't even know Schmid was in town 'till our statehouse man asked this afternoon if we were covering him," Raus said. "Usually we get a couple days' notice. Is this a secret trip or what?"

I kicked Whine, who was about to tell Raus the whole itinerary.

I didn't care if they knew about us working in their town, but it was no use giving the opposition a road map for the rest of the week if they decided to try to play some catch-up.

"Oh, we just happened on the chance to do some art for a big piece on senior citizens," I lied. "We're on the way back home tomorrow."

That last was true, because home was en route to Morrow and Schmid's first stop Wednesday. We drove back to the capital Tuesday, and stopped in the office, where Whine vanished to process his pictures and I went to see Swift.

"I'm not sure this is going to pay off," I told him. "So far, Schmid has been doing just what Goldberg said he would. No unscheduled stops—nothing that looks strange."

Swift had this habit of fluffing his beard when people talked to him. "Well, how about these private meetings? What's going on in them?" Swift asked.

"I don't know, they wouldn't let us interview the people who were in those sessions. They didn't even give out their names."

"Wouldn't let you? Didn't give out names?" Swift was incensed. "See here, old man, stop accepting what these people hand you and do some reporting! Have you ever heard of staking out a meeting and following people who leave it? Have you ever heard of asking other people in the area who that was that got a private audience with the governor? Use some initiative for God's sake!"

"Look, Mr. Swift, I thought this was a good idea when you

sent us out to follow the governor. But it looks like it's just what he says . . . an inspection trip and handshaking excursion. I don't think we're going to find out what he's up to—if he's up to anything—by tagging along with him all over the state.

"Why don't we save some money by calling this off, and I'll do some checking at the statehouse and with some of the politicians. . . ."

"Let me worry about the money, if you don't mind. And, you'll do some checking over there and with the politicians when you get back, Wartovsky. Both of us had a notion—a hunch I think you Yanks call it—that Schmid was running around the state for some reason he wasn't talking about. Now we have a chance to watch him in action, and you want to retreat to your comfortable statehouse pressroom and sit on your duff making telephone calls. Get out and do some legwork; that's the way you get news."

Back on the road we went, arriving at Morrow Wednesday morning ahead of the governor. Whine took the car to do some pictures of the water and soil conservation project (the object of the governor's visit), and I dropped in at the courthouse to talk to a former state legislator who was now the local district attorney.

Bill Phlager ushered me right into his office and poured me a cup of coffee. He was in the governor's party, but I had always found him to be an independent cuss and an honest one.

"Yeah, I'm surprised old Schmid is coming here. Our soil and water project is eight years old and so far as I know is doing very well. If he was running for reelection, I could understand why he'd want to be seen with a successful project, but he isn't running, and you tell me he's doing nothing to attract the press on this trip. I'm curious too. Let me know what you find out."

The manager of the soil and water project was more than curious; he was downright nervous. The governor had called him directly to say he was coming for a tour and that he wanted to talk to some of the farmers who were supposed to be benefiting from the project.

"You're damn right they're benefiting," the manager said as we waited next to a drainage pump shed for the governor to arrive. "Normal rainfall was eroding this valley at a terrible rate until we started the project, and any unusually wet season was scouring the soil down to hardpan. Ten more years and this country would have been unfarmable."

The governor and Moose showed up and the manager scurried off to greet him. Whine and I followed as he showed Schmid through the mechanical works of the project and ushered him into the small headquarters building where several local farmers waited. Once more, we were cut out, but this time I argued with the governor about the freeze.

"How can we cover the news if you exclude us?" I asked. "You're supposed to be doing state business and the sunshine laws say that has to be done in public."

Schmid scowled at that. "They say state business is supposed to be done in public, but they also allow for executive communications," he said. "I'm making no decisions in these meetings; I'm simply listening to people who have a unique insight into state-financed projects—and that is tantamount to staff meetings in my office at the Capitol. Those are closed because I want to hear candid opinions without the media hanging on every word. . . . and this is the same. If you want to make something out of it, complain to the attorney general."

We sat and waited for the meeting to end, and Whine and I each got the name of one of the farmers as they left the project grounds. The man I talked to, Ivan Carver, said he had urgent business in town and couldn't talk, and Whine's guy, William Reckel, said he had nothing to say about the meeting. When we got back to our car, Moose was sitting in the driver's seat.

"Hey, Wartovsky, this car has something wrong with it," Moose announced with a big grin on his face.

"What do you mean? It works fine."

"Maybe, but the gear shift lever is loose," the big cop said. He took hold of the lever and without even grunting, ripped it off the steering column.

"Hey! What the hell are you doing, you ape!"

Moose got out of the car and grabbed my shirt. "You know better than to speak disrespectfully to an officer of the law, buster. What you want to do now is get your car fixed."

As he spoke, Moose took hold of the mirror on the driver's side door and wrenched it off. Then he walked around the rear of the car and kicked out the glass in the tail light. "You can't drive around this state without proper mirrors or lights, either. I ought to ticket you now, but for an old friend, this is just a warning." Moose stalked off.

"I'm going to report this," I yelled after Moose.

He walked back to the car. "Feel free," he said. "I was with the governor all the time we were here. He'll say so and whose word is going to carry more weight?" He turned and lumbered toward the building where the governor was just finishing his meetings.

"Now how are we going to keep up with the governor?" Whine asked. "You should know better than to call that big ape a big ape."

One of the farmers who had been talking to Schmid came out of the project building then, and I asked him where the nearest garage was.

"Back in town," he said. When I explained our car would have to be towed in and asked for a lift, he agreed to drive one of us into town in his pickup.

I climbed into the truck, and we started toward Morrow— about three miles down the road.

Remembering what Swift had said, and seeing a chance for an interview, I asked, "How did your meeting with the governor go?"

"Passable," the farmer said.

"Did you have any complaints or suggestions about the conservation project?"

"Nope. Project works fine. User charges are high, but fair, I guess."

"Well, what did you two have to talk about?"

"Kenny."

"Kenny?"

"My boy. Up at Watertown. He's coming up for pardon this week."

"You talked about a pardon for your son?"

"Oh, it's all set."

"You know he's going to get a pardon?"

"I'm pretty sure. The governor said he'd look into it."

"How did you happen to be one of the people to talk with the governor today? Was it just a coincidence?"

"No coincidence. I got a call from somebody last week telling me to show up at the project today."

"Did the call say anything about Kenny?"

"Nope. Just to show up. But I had a good idea that's what it was about, the pardon hearing being this Friday and all. Then when the governor said he wanted to talk to us separately, I figured Kenny was the reason."

Careful now. Ask the questions carefully.

"Did you bring up Kenny when you saw the governor?"

"Sure, he's my boy and I need him on the place."

"What did the governor say?"

"Said he hadn't had a chance to really study the case, what with the problems he was having paying off his campaign debt from the last election."

The governor's last campaign had cost him $400,000, and I knew for a fact that he had collected at least half a million for it. Even his campaign finance report showed a surplus.

"Did he ask you for a contribution?"

"Not right out. But I figured it couldn't hurt to offer one, and he seemed right happy and relieved when I said I could help out with five hundred dollars or so. Right then, he said he thought it ought to be possible to do something to help Kenny."

Bingo and bull's-eye. I suddenly realized I was on to a story that—don't laugh—could blow the lid right off the Capitol.

I spent the rest of the short trip into town assuring the farmer, Fred Rice, that I was only interested in a human interest story about a man's fight to free his son (so I lied again) and getting the details about Kenny's trip up the river two years before.

It was one of those typical stories: The kid got beered up on a Saturday night, got into a brawl at a roadhouse over some trifle, and ended up crowning another guy with a beer bottle. He'd had similar trouble before, so the county judge sent him away for three to five years on the aggravated assault conviction.

Rice was able to make his farm pay only if he had Kenny's help, and he was so pathetically grateful for the chance to get his son back before the spring planting that he seemed oblivious to the fact he was involving himself in bribery of the state's highest official.

As he left me at the garage, I told him I'd like to come back after Kenny was out and talk some more. He seemed amenable.

I rode the tow truck back out to the project and Whine was there alone with the car. The governor had left and it took the best part of the day for the garage to scrounge up parts and install them.

By the time we got underway, we figured the governor had completed his scheduled stop at Severs, so we headed for the next town on the list, Manville. I didn't tell Whine what farmer Rice had told me, but said it was really important to get the names of the people the governor talked to the next day.

That night, I called Swift and told him that the car had

cost $198 in repairs (on the company credit card). I also told him what the farmer had said. He was unhappy about the first, but got real excited about the second and said to stay on the story. We were not to follow Schmid to Watertown on Friday for the pardon hearing in order to avoid tipping him that we were on to something.

The announced object of the visit to Manville was to inspect a new highway bypass and bridge over the Soocatchee River. We got to the project early and, after badgering the engineer in charge, Whine got out on the half-finished bridge to take some pictures of Schmid as he surveyed the work.

When they arrived and the governor was escorted to the bridge approach, I sidled up to Moose.

"None of that strong-arm stuff today, Moose. My photographer is out there on the bridge with a telephoto lens and it's focused on you, big boy."

Moose grunted. "I'm just doing my job and what I'm told. You stay away from the governor and I'll stay away from you."

This time there were only three locals waiting to see the governor, and I stopped the first one out.

"Did you have a good visit with the governor, sir?"

"You're who?"

"Wartovsky, *Capital Register & Press.*"

"Nothing to say to you. Private meeting. The governor said you'd be snooping out here."

"Will you give me your name?"

"It's none of your damn business."

"Do you happen to have a relative in prison?"

The man stepped up to me and grabbed my coat. "That's even less of your damn business, mister. One more question and I deck you."

The second man out strode swiftly to his car, ignoring my efforts to stop him. The third person was a woman, and it appeared she had been crying.

"Ma'am, can I speak with you a moment?"

"Oh, please go away. I haven't anything to say."

"But maybe I can help."

"How? You haven't got six hundred dollars in your pocket to spare, have you?" She got into her car and pulled away.

Whine was off the bridge by then and packing his gear into the trunk. "I got shots of you with that first man and the woman. Did you get their names?"

Of course, I hadn't but Whine's question gave me an idea. "Hey, what's the closest place you can get the film processed?"

"Maybe back in town, at the weekly there if they have a darkroom. But I can't work good in any place except my own."

"No time, we've got to try to get names for those people."

The weekly editor was Chester Lewis, and he didn't get many visits from fellow newsies. He was hospitable and more than eager to help. I lied to him too, telling him we were doing a story on the governor's visit and needed identifications on our pictures for the captions.

I whispered to Whine to crop me out of the pictures and sat down to wait. He was out in thirty minutes with a set of photographs of the first man I talked to, the woman, and a blurry side shot of the man who refused to stop and talk.

Lewis knew the woman, Mrs. Ned Willink, and said the man who had grabbed me was Thomas Weller, a local auto dealer. He thought he could identify the man who had fled as a George Canther. And he gave me the link I needed without being asked.

"That's strange," he said. "Her husband and Weller's brother were involved in a mail-order fraud case a couple of years ago. But what does that have to do with the highway?"

"I don't know for sure, Chet," I said. "But if I find out, you'll be the first to know." Another lie, but I did owe Lewis for the help.

We got back to the capital late that night. Whine dropped me at my apartment and he took the company car home.

The next morning I went to the office and presented Swift with what we had. He combed his beard with his fingers for a while and said, "It's thin as gruel, old boy, but you obviously have gotten a whiff of a big one. I'm not sure how we're going to handle it yet, but go out and get everything about this down . . . on paper, not in the computer. Meanwhile, I'll make sure we get a complete story on the pardon hearings from the wires."

I went into the storeroom, unearthed one of the typewriters that had been retired by the advent of the computer, and began transcribing my notes and everything I had in my memory from the trip.

I was about two-thirds finished when Swift came over with a piece of yellow teletype paper.

"What was the name of the young man whose father was going to contribute to the governor's campaign debt?" Swift asked.

"Kenny Rice."

Swift pointed to the last paragraph of the National Press story:

Pardon applications denied included John Wismer, who was sentenced to life six years ago for the murder of a Rockland County deputy sheriff, and Timothy Selig, a Spring City man, convicted of multiple rape. Others rejected in bids for freedom were Ned Willink, Manville, sentenced for mail fraud; Meyer Knowles, Wright City, convicted of burglary; and Kenneth Rice, a Morrow youth, serving a term for assault.

CHAPTER 6

"It appears, Wartovsky, as if you've come a cropper," Swift said as he pointed to the wire story. "The man whose father was going to buy a pardon from the governor is going to remain in prison."

I was thunderstruck. If Kenny Rice wasn't freed, the whole theory that Schmid was on the take seemed to totter. Could I have misunderstood Fred Rice?

I looked at the top of the National Press wire story, and I felt better.

WATERTOWN (NP)—Gov. A. Pinckney Schmid today granted pardons to six state prison inmates—including an elderly man who shot a teenager who had played a Halloween prank on him.

August Hantz, 76, was convicted three years ago of firing a .22 caliber rifle at a group of youths who had left a brimming garbage can tipped against his front door and rung the bell. James O'Riordan, 16, was killed by the shot.

Hantz told a jury youngsters in his inner-city neighborhood had been harrassing him and his wife for years, but he had meant to fire the gun into the air only to frighten the youths.

The governor said in a prepared statement that he had pardoned Hantz because the man had shown remorse, and because the incident appeared to have been a tragic accident.

Also freed by gubernatorial action were:

56

Morris Carver, Sepperville, serving a term for setting fire to a neighbor's barn as the climax of a long feud. Schmid said the evidence in the case was circumstantial and there had been some question of community hostility to Carver when the jury was chosen.

Edward Stampel, a former clerk in the city records office, convicted of embezzlement. The governor said subsequent legal action demonstrated that Stampel had been following orders of a superior who was profiting from the actions.

Pardons also went to Samuel Tucker, rural Severs; Reed Weller, Manville; and Glenn Lightly, suburban Westover.

I was excited. "Look, there are two men here whose names are the same as people we talked to," I said and told Swift about our contacts with Ivan Carver and Thomas Weller during the week. "I don't know what happened with Kenny Rice, but here are two more leads."

Swift agreed. He told me to head back to Morrow and Manville the next Monday, and said he would send Whine to the city with the pictures he took at the senior citizen centers to see if he could get identifications.

Whine whined, complaining that he wasn't paid to be an investigative reporter, but Swift gave him an offer he couldn't refuse. "I know you're not a reporter, Mr. Tandee, but if you can't see your way clear to taking on this task, you're not a photographer, either. Not at this paper, anyway."

Monday morning, Whine, equipped with a tape recorder, was off to the city and I for the sticks. By midafternoon, I was driving down a country road outside Morrow looking for a mail box marked Rice. With directions from a filling station at the turnoff from the state highway, I found the mail box and a very muscular looking young woman who was just emptying it.

I got out of the car and asked, "Is this the Rice place?"

The woman, at least five feet ten and a good 170 pounds, replied, "Yes. You have business?"

"I'm Bob Wartovsky from the *Capital* . . ."

"From the capital? Daddy hasn't got anything for you. He told you on the phone last Thursday he wasn't going to pay a cent to you even if Kenny did have to stay in jail."

"Whoa. I'm from the *Capital Register & Press*. I talked to Mr. Rice on Wednesday."

"Oh, the reporter. Well, what Daddy told you didn't happen. He isn't going to pay any bribes to anybody. Besides, Kenny is eligible for parole in six or seven months."

"Is your father home? I want to ask him some more about his talk with the governor."

"That piss-ant! If I had gone up there I would have turned him in right then. But we don't want to have any more trouble, and Daddy doesn't want to talk about it anymore. He said too much to you last week. I could have ended up alone here with two men in prison."

"But that's it. The governor ought to be put in jail."

"Well, somebody else is going to have to put him there. This family has had enough trouble." She reached over and grabbed me by the shoulder, whirled me around, and shoved me back toward the car.

I'm not all that macho, but I'm not used to being woman-handled either. I started back toward the girl—she looked about twenty—and suddenly found myself lifted by the belt in the back of my pants and deposited in the car. It probably was lucky I left the door open; she might have chucked me through the window.

I thought about pressing the point for about nine seconds. The girl was standing in the middle of the dirt road leading to the farm and looked like she was prepared to stand there even if I tried to drive right at her. I put the car into reverse and headed back toward Morrow.

Bill Phlager came out of his office into the waiting room as soon as his secretary told him on the intercom that I was there.

"I expected to be seeing or hearing from you. I've got someone in the office right now, but if you can wait, I think we've got some things to talk about."

It took about forty minutes. I used the time to find a pay phone and call Swift to tell him about the meeting with Rice's Amazonian daughter and my decision to go to Phlager.

Swift didn't much like it. "You should have tried first to contact that other man—Carver, isn't it? If you get the authorities into this, we can lose the jump we have on everyone."

I called information for Ivan Carver. The phone was answered by a woman who said he was out, and she didn't know when he would be back. I went back to Phlager's office just as the door to the inner sanctum opened and Ivan Carver, looking wan, exited with another man. Carver started as he saw me standing in the D.A.'s outer office, paused, but then scuttled out.

Phlager came to the door. "Come in, Bob."

As I sat in a seat next to his desk, Phlager said, "As you can see, I didn't wait for you to call. When I heard about the pardons Friday, I phoned Carver and told him to get down here today. He brought his lawyer—and good thing too.

"Now, what have you got?"

Phlager listened as I recounted last week's events, interrupting to press me for details when I told him of seeing Carver at the meeting with the governor. He jotted notes on a legal pad as I recounted the conversation with Rice and my encounter with Rice's daughter.

"Well, Bob, you've just filled in the pieces of a puzzle that some of us have been working on for almost a year. I knew Carver and Rice were at the project because Bill Reckel came in here Wednesday and told me he had seen them.

"He went there wondering why in hell he had been invited because he quit farming five years ago. But he got the same kind of call Rice did and went to find out what it was all about it. He said Schmid started out asking him about the project, but all of a sudden brought up the fact that he was presiding over the pardon hearing and looked at him as if he expected Bill to pick up on it.

"Well, Bill's brother-in-law is Meyer Knowles, who I put away a couple of years ago for a run of burglaries that had the farmers in the county up in arms. He waited for weekends when the families all went to town or church and looted them—we found enough TVs, microwaves, and other stuff at his place to stock Sears. The funny thing was, one of the television sets was Reckel's, and the last thing he was interested in was getting Meyer out of the slammer. When he didn't make a pitch, the governor ended the talk and Bill came to see me.

"That's why I called Carver in, but he claimed he talked to the governor only about the project and that Morris's name never came up. I didn't really have anything from what Bill told me, but if I can get Fred Rice to talk, we might just have ole Pinckney by the balls.

"I'll tell you something else, but you'll have to take it on background—no attribution to me. The attorney general has been building a case against Schmid ever since he issued a couple real smelly pardons last year. I know some other county D.A.'s have been alerted too, and if I'm not mistaken, there'll be a grand jury impaneled soon."

"What can I write?"

"Depends what else you have. You know Schmid talked to three people here who had relatives up for pardon, you identified two—Weller and Willink—over at Manville, and I bet you can make the same kind of connection at Severs and in the city. If I were you, I'd talk to the A.G. before writing anything, but I'll be glad to call him and vouch for the help you've given here."

I could see a lot more work ahead. I thanked Phlager and went back to the pay phone for another call to Swift. I had to wait for him to come on the line, and when he did he was one excited Brit.

"Get back here instantly, Bob, this thing is breaking right now. Tandee got lucky. He found the wife of one of the men who was pardoned, Stampel, I believe, and after he told her that there were rumors of pardons being sold for five and six hundred dollars, she blew up and told him—on tape—if you can believe it, old man—that her family paid one thousand two hundred dollars, and she wanted to know why they were charged twice the going price.

"We transcribed the tape over the phone and Cindy Korth took it over to the attorney general at the Capitol. He wouldn't comment on the record but told her he'd be having a press conference tomorrow.

"Give me a quick rundown on anything you have and then get back here. We're going big with this."

It took me about twenty minutes to dictate what I had from Phlager, and then I spent two hours on the road trying to frame the story in my mind. There was no need. When I got back to the paper, Swift had started the main story with a triple byline (my name, Cindy Korth, and Rip Tandee), a sidebar with the Stampel transcription, and laid out headlines and pictures for a three-page spread that would have done justice to the end of a World War.

"Why don't you just put Granville Swift on the story?" I asked after glancing over the layout. "Seems to me you don't need me for anything here."

"Oh, don't get your nose out of joint, old boy," Swift replied. "We've got a paper to get out and there's no time to stand on ceremony. Now, pick up where I've left off on the main story and finish it up in another two columns. This has to be read over by the bloody lawyers before we can go with it."

I sat down at the computer and read what Swift had written. It was feverish prose, but careful—never quite accusing Schmid of taking bribes while leaving no real doubt. All I had to do with the story was fill in some of the details of the trip and weave in the background of the investigation from Phlager.

After an hour, I was finished and pushed the computer file button. Then I picked up the phone and called Chet Lewis in Manville to repay a favor.

"Thanks a lot, Bob, but you didn't have to hurry," Lewis said after I filled him in. "This is a weekly, remember, and if the Second Coming happened on Monday, we'd still print it on Thursday. But this will give us some time to develop the local angles."

By that time, the pages were dummied and the front was, to say the least, eye-catching. Across the top, over a file picture of the governor, was a headline in three-inch type, printed red:

GOV. SCHMID: ARE
PARDONS FOR SALE?

Below the photo, just in case anyone wondered about the question, was another headline of the same size in black:

CONVICTS' KIN
PAY UP TO $1200

And finally, taking up the rest of the tabloid page, a third headline in slightly smaller type:

STATE A.G.
SETS PROBE

Page two was devoted to pictures of the men who were pardoned, plus Kenny Rice, Meyer Knowles, and Ned Willink. The best touch was a shot dug out of the files showing the governor touring a cell block at the state pen.

The story started on page three, and I had to admit it was a masterpiece of its type:

Scandal in the form of an alleged pardon-selling scheme Monday hit the administration of Gov. A. P. Schmid like a tornado off the prairie.

State Attorney General Markham Lee was expected to announce today that evidence of the scheme, much of it gathered by the *Capital Register & Press,* would be submitted to a grand jury. Sources said some of the state's highest-ranking officials could be implicated. "Heads will roll," a Capitol insider predicted. "Some big shots are going to be going to jail."

(I asked Cindy the next day where that quote had come from. "Right here," she said. "Swift showed me the copy and when I said I didn't have any such quote, told me, 'Well, that's what Capitol insiders will be saying when they see this.'")

Rumors of a pardon-selling conspiracy have been under official investigation for nearly a year, but it was investigative reporting by this newspaper's staff that broke it open in the last week.

A statement, recorded by a *Capital Press & Register* staff photographer, from the wife of a man pardoned only last Friday, provided the spark that impelled the attorney general to act. It was understood that other key evidence, assembled by several law enforcement officers around the state, also has been submitted to the state's highest legal officer.

"There's too much smoke here for there not to be a fire," one official said. "We've got the goods and more is coming."

(Cindy said the "official" was the same person as the "Capitol insider." She told me, "Swift was mad as hell at me for not getting some quotes from Lee. He just went ahead and made it up.")

Efforts by this newspaper to get comment on the matter from Governor Schmid were unavailing. Phillip

Goldberg, the governor's spokesman, said, "We haven't got anything on that, and if we did I doubt we would be giving it to your paper. Your vendetta against this administration is well known."

Shigetsu Shiu, publisher of the *Capital Register & Press*, replied to Goldberg's charge in a statement: "This newspaper has vendettas against no one. We are interested in the truth and under the First Amendment we intend to publish it when we find it."

("Swift wrote that too," Cindy said. "Shiu wasn't even in town. I heard he flew down to Chicago . . . hey, did you know he was a pilot?")

The recorded statement by Mrs. Helen Stampel, whose husband had been serving a five-year term for embezzlement from a city records office, was turned over to the attorney general's office by the *Capital Register & Press*.

In it, Mrs. Stampel said her family had paid $1,200 to secure a pardon for Edward Stampel last week. She said she was contacted by a high state official at a center for senior citizens and told that a "contribution" of that amount would help Stampel's cause at a pardon hearing held Friday at the state penitentiary in Watertown.

This was the point where I picked up the story Swift had started. It went on to recount the Rice episode, substituting "a high state official" for Schmid's name, and summarized the other encounters with relatives of prisoners during the week, plus the background provided by Phlager. Swift told me, "We can't name Schmid in this story, but we can do everything to point at him."

I was surprised how easy it was, with the start Swift provided, to tar the governor head to foot without identifying him. Swift said after I finished, "Good job, old fellow. With a little experience, I think you might go somewhere in this business."

Of course, we were sued. The governor filed a libel action before the sun set on Tuesday. But also, of course, the suit was put on hold when the state Assembly voted to impeach the governor, and a special grand jury handed up an indictment as long as Wilt Chamberlain's arm against the Honorable A. Pinckney Schmid all in the same week.

We printed a small story about dismissal of the suit in the back of the same edition that was led by this full page of headlines:

PARDONGATE IMPEACHMENT!
GOOD-BYE SCHMID

SENATE CONVICTS GOVERNOR
LT. GOV. TAKES REINS

EX-GOV. BRIBE TRIAL
SET NEXT MONTH

CAP R&P LAUDED
BY SOLONS

And to think it all began with a dog crapping on the Capitol floor.

CHAPTER 7

Whine and I were newsroom heroes in the two months after our trip while the Schmid story was running its course. Shiu had us up to his office for pictures to be sent to *Editor & Publisher* and said something about both of us seeing the paper's appreciation in our paychecks. When that didn't happen after a couple of weeks, I asked Swift.

"Bad timing, old man. I wrote up an increase order for thirty dollars more a week for both of you, but it got to his desk the same day as a memo from the auditor questioning the auto repair in Morrow. It was all I could do to keep the little beggar from docking your pay.

"As you doubtless have noticed, Shiu is no veteran of this business. He told me once he liked newspaper publishing because the raw material for the product is free, and it simply is beyond him that it costs money to gather news. He thinks it can be picked up on the street, like candy wrappers or cigarette ends.

"And by the way, he also got a touch huffy about your restaurant bills in the city. Said it appeared to him you two were trying to bring economic recovery to the brewing and sausage industries all by yourselves."

With such an enlightened attitude, I let it drop. Besides, I got the equivalent of a fifteen- or twenty-dollar-a-week pay increase for the free dinners I was invited to by civic groups for several months.

There also was talk about entering our work for some big

prizes, but it was becoming clear to me that the *CR&P*'s reputation in the industry was going down faster than any muckraking coup could boost it. We still were giving big play to the weirdest crime, sex, and mayhem stories that came over the wire and, within two months after we went tabloid, we could have gone head-to-headline with any of those London or New York papers that try to knock your socks off every morning with their front page.

Just a couple Swift came up with: A story about a judge who permitted identification of a police informant who was later shot—the headline was:

STOOLIE FINGERED
BY JUDGE; SLAIN

A piece about a crazed man who stripped off his clothes in a city park and then shot a policeman who tried to subdue him:

NUDE NUT
KILLS COP

The prize may have been the story about the jail inmate who tried to escape by sneaking into the back of a trash truck and found himself being pressed into a bale of "solid waste":

BREAKOUT FAILS,
CON—PACTED

We didn't get any prizes, but we did get some of what the management took to be flattering attention. Frank Sanders and his kids were one such manifestation of the respect—or maybe curiosity—that the new *Capital Register & Press* got.

Swift called me into his cubicle one morning and, in the tones of a prosecuting attorney, demanded: "You know this Professor Frank Sanders?"

I didn't have the foggiest notion what he was getting at, but I did know Sanders casually and said so.

"Well, you've got him. Shiu informs me this Sanders is bringing an entire bloody journalism class from the state university during the semester break to observe us, and that they are particularly interested in you and your work—so as of next week, old man, you are the nanny for Sanders and his brats."

"How long is this going to be? I've got some pieces I'm working on that won't keep too long."

"A week, maybe two. They're making a short course out of us or some absurd thing. If you can do your work and shepherd them around as well, fine. But Shiu wants them attended to . . . thinks it will polish our image or something. That's your primary assignment until you can pack them off."

So it was, with a clean shirt and tie and a dirty hangover, I greeted Sanders and his flock in the newsroom the following Monday. There were five boys and three girls, whoops, women, including the prettiest young thing I have seen that early in the morning since I got lucky a couple years ago on a Club Med week.

My luck. The lady I liked was Sanders' daughter. And Sanders, although going to flab, was football-sized, about six feet three and 230 pounds or more. He also was a shuffler and scratcher—constantly in motion while he talked in a Jimmy Stewart kind of drawl.

"W'all, it's mighty fine of you to meet us . . . ah, here this morning, ah, Bob. We're right happy for the chance to talk to you and maybe even watch you work if we won't get in the way.

"Lemme introduce my kids. Here's my l'il daughter, Lizbeth, and Lou Strazzi, Carl Swing, Abe Blunk, Mary Dear, Ty-rone Flowers, Jennie Gaffney, and Jimmy Witt. My best students, Bob, and it was their choice to come down here to sit in at the *Register & Press*."

I suggested we adjourn to Angelina's coffee shop down the

street for some warm sustenance and get acquainted. We pushed a couple of tables together and spent most of the morning talking. That is, I sucked up coffee and tried to give semi-intelligent and reasonably civil responses as Sanders talked and the kids peppered me with questions.

They were most interested in the Schmid story, and as I explained how it developed, Sanders added professorial footnotes.

"How did you know the governor was up to something crooked?" a runty kid already starting to show thinning hair (a natural desk man—city editor material, if he was mean enough) asked.

"We had no idea. We just were trying to find out why he suddenly was traveling around the state when before you couldn't get him out of the capital with a nuclear blast."

Sanders interjected: "Aberrant behavior. Look for something that is out of the ordinary and find out what caused it. That's the way y'all find news—the kind some folks don't want you to find."

"Why didn't you write a story about the trooper trying to scare you off when it happened? Why didn't you scorch his ass?" This from as sweet-looking and petite a blonde as you could fantasize taking home to Mom.

"We weren't after Moose. By that time we had an idea that Schmid was on the take, and we didn't want to alert anyone we were on it."

Sanders: "Establish your priorities. Don't fire your ammunition at a little ole jaybird if you've got a chance to bring down a big buzzard."

"What made you think of sending the photographer back to the city to get identifications on his pictures of the people waiting to see the governor?" From a tall, serious-looking red-headed guy. (He looked like a pipe-smoker and potential *New York Times* man.)

"Hell, I didn't think of it. The managing editor sent Tandee."

Sanders: "The editor looks at the whole picture. The reporter may be looking at only one piece. You may not think so being as reporters are the glamour boys and gals, but the ole editor is usually far more important to the process than the reporter."

I saw my opportunity: "Why don't we go back to the paper and see if Mr. Swift has a few minutes to talk to you. He certainly had as much to do with this as Tandee and I did."

I figured Swift wasn't going to be happy about talking to a bunch of kids, so I didn't call ahead. We walked back to the paper and bearded the bearded one on his glass-sided cage. He was poring over a stack of wire service stories looking for something wild and weird enough to make a front page headline.

"I'm busy. I told you to take care of these people," he muttered as I waved Sanders and the kids in.

"Shiu said this would polish our image. Besides, they've got managing editor questions. You want me to tell them how this paper judges newsworthiness?"

Teeth showing in a hairy smile, Swift told the kids clustered around his desk, "Welcome to the *Capital Register & Press*. It is our pleasure to have you here to observe a newspaper being made. Please feel free to ask me anything."

A husky, dark-haired young woman standing in front got in the first question, a low, wicked curve that would have done justice to a Sam Donaldson or a Helen Thomas:

"How come you've turned the *Register & Press* into a tabloid scandal sheet? It used to be a serious paper and now it looks like something you'd buy at a supermarket checkout."

Swift unfolded from his chair and towered over everybody in the room but Sanders. Looking like Charlton Heston getting ready to part the Dead Sea, he fixed the young woman with a glare.

"Scandal sheet? See here, my lady, you've got some strange ideas of what a real newspaper is. Maybe Professor Sanders here has told you that *The New York Times* or the

Christian Science Monitor are what newspapers are supposed to be, but don't you believe for a minute that they are the real standard in this business. And yes, I said business. You may think you're studying to become professionals, but you'll find out what newspapers need and pay for is craftsmen—people who know how to make a product that sells to readers and to advertisers."

The girl wasn't cowed: "Well, Mr. Swift, I understand that your reputation has gotten so bad you don't have a chance to win the Pulitzer Prize even with the Schmid story—which may be the best exposé of the year."

"Pulitzer, is it?" Swift was getting red in the face. He turned to the shelf behind him and pulled down a thick book.

"Perhaps we should refer to history. Your teachers will tell you that Pulitzer's *World* was the epitome of great journalism, but in point of fact it was as rowdy a piece of work as you'll find anywhere."

Swift opened the book to a marked page. "Now listen to what Joseph Pulitzer told the staff of the *New York World* at their first meeting: 'Gentlemen, you realize that a change has taken place at the *World*. Heretofore you have all been living in the parlor and taking baths every day. Now I wish you to understand that in future you are all walking down the Bowery.'

"They were in a circulation war then, and Pulitzer was determined to win it. Those old papers were louder and more raucous than we ever thought of being, and they were ready to manufacture the news if the real thing wasn't exciting enough for them. Sometimes they even fabricated pictures.

"Oh, yes, your big papers have become respectable and sanctimonious enough today, but look at their market positions. Most of them are monopolies and a lot of them even own their so-called television competition. It's when there is hand-to-hand combat on the news racks that newspapering challenges the clever.

"Now, you want to know why we pursued the governor? Because it was a good story . . . one that would make people say—what is it, Wartovsky?—'Gee, whiz.' You have heard of Joseph Medill Patterson? Creator of the largest circulation newspaper in America. He was asked what made the *Daily News* a success, and his answer was, 'Hijinks in high places.' It works every time, right down to the *Washington Post* and Watergate.

"Perhaps we did do a service to the people of this state who elected that lout, but that wasn't why we got into it. The First Amendment you Americans are so proud of doesn't say the press is supposed to protect the public from its own blunders, even if that is what its authors intended. It does say the American press is to be free . . . and that means free to do whatever its proprietors want it to do."

Swift subsided and sat down glumly. The kids, who had heard a somewhat different view of the high purposes of press freedom from their instructors, stared at the floor, none willing to ask another question that might provoke a diatribe. Sanders, for the first time that day, didn't have an interpretation handy.

Recovering his cool, Swift looked up at me and said, "And now I think you ought to tour our state-of-the-art newsroom and publishing plant. Mr. Wartovsky, please show the group around the newsroom and see if someone in the shop can give them a rundown on the composing and printing facilities. Oh, and step back here for a moment when you can, Bob."

I herded the group out and turned them over to the composing room boss, who was as enthusiastic about dropping everything and becoming a tour guide as your average NFL tackle would be serving high tea. I went back to Swift's office.

"The next time you spring something like that on me

you'll be covering church dinners for the state page," Swift growled when I came in. "I bloody well got the wind up, and if Shiu hears about it, he'll have a shit fit."

"Well, you certainly gave it to them with the bark on," I said.

"It won't happen again, old boy. Now, did you say you knew Sanders?"

"From a journalism school seminar on statehouse reporting at the university. He moderated and we had a couple of drinks after. He used to work back East and we traded some old-timer stories."

"You can bet your life he worked in the East. I didn't connect the name until I saw the face. Frank Sanders was the hottest snoop in New York twenty years ago, before some twit invented the term investigative journalism. He had the politicians in the city and Albany quaking and then he quit at the top of his game, saying he had enough of long hours and low pay.

"Now then, Wartovsky, what in the hell is he doing here?"

"Hell, how should I know? Teaching his kids. You think he has something else in mind?"

"I don't know either. But I want you to keep your eyes open and your mouth shut about the executives and the management of this newspaper. That's the rest of your assignment—and try to keep them out of the building. Take them to cover the state highway commission or something."

I thought that over as I went to the back shop to retrieve Sanders and the kids. Why was Swift so nervous about a journalism professor?

Sanders took me aside after I introduced the kids to the newsroom and found a computer terminal they could try out.

"Bob, old buddy, what do you think of your new bosses?" he asked.

"What's to think? They're running the paper and we do it their way or check out. It's kind of wild, but it sure isn't as boring as it was when Morgan and Fargo ran the show. We got to calling it the 'Register and Suppress' toward the end."

"D'ya know anything about Shiu? Or Swift?"

"Not much. Shiu doesn't know much about the editorial side, but Swift sure does. He gets bizarre at times, but he knows news."

"Oh, yes," Sanders said. "Granville Swift is, or was, one of the hottest yellow editors in the world. When I worked back East, he already was a legend. He's edited tabs in London, Sydney, and New York and raised circulation and hell everywhere he's gone. I don't know the whole story, but one of my old friends wrote me that Swift took on a Boston paper about six years ago that he couldn't help, and it turned him into a kind of monomaniac. Ruined his marriage and his health. The story went around that he got burned out and was let go.

"I heard from another guy that 'burned out' was something of a euphemism. According to him, Swift got some idea in his head that there was a tabloid story out there to end 'em all and plain cracked up looking for it. Kind of a search for an unholy grail, I guess. So far as I know, he hasn't worked since."

Sanders paused and looked at me hard.

"Now then, Bob, what in the hell is he doing here?"

CHAPTER 8

Great. Now I had Swift asking me what Sanders was up to and Sanders cross-examining me about Swift. I personally didn't give diddley-damn what either was doing, and I told Sanders just that.

Sanders took me by the arm and walked me out of the paper and down the block to the Next Door. He prodded me all the way to the dimly lit back booth, ordered a Heilemann's for himself and a Stroh's for me (a remarkable memory—that was the first time we'd had a drink together for several years) and sat for at least a full minute staring at me.

Finally, he said, "I'm gonna take a chance. Bob, have you ever heard of The Center for Inquiry?"

"Sure. It's the outfit that was set up a couple of years back to back up investigative reporters—organizes investigations itself sometimes."

"That's right. It's a clearinghouse for investigative journalism, and it did run that special team investigation down South after Bo Glassman disappeared. That's its public face."

"There's more?"

"There is. I'm gonna tell you about it and I hope you'll keep it dark—whether or not you decide to help me."

"Now, wait a minute, Frank. I'm not making any promises about anything. I've been at this business too long to let myself get mousetrapped by anyone."

"Good. Just hear me out and then decide." Sanders took a long pull on his beer.

"CFI is funded by a group of foundations. Most of the money goes for the work you and most everyone else in the business knows about. But it also has what is called an 'executive endowment.' That's a sum of money, a considerable sum, I'm told, that is earmarked for investigating possible corruption within the news business itself. Bribe-taking by reporters, kickbacks to editors, taking or giving favors . . . that kind of thing.

"If it finds something that stinks in a news operation, it turns the information over to the employers of the bad apple involved and walks away from it. CFI doesn't go any further with it, even if the people in charge don't follow up. That way there's no whiff of vigilantism or of trying to set up as some overseer of the press's morals.

"There's one more area the endowment works in and this is even more sensitive. When a paper or a station changes hands and there are indications that the new ownership isn't on the up and up, CFI tries to check it out. If it finds something fishy, it turns the information over to one of the professional groups in the field."

Now I could guess what was coming. Sanders lifted his glass again but kept staring hard at me.

"I've been out of the business for twelve years, but I do keep my hand in with occasional jobs for the Center. So, What we have is that CFI has been hearing rumors that the *Capital Register & Press* may have been taken over by the syndicate, and because I used to have some pretty good contacts on the fringes of that neighborhood, they've asked me to look into it."

"This stuff about bringing these kids here to observe the paper is just bullshit?"

"Oh, not entirely. We do field trips like this all the time. But this one also is a bit of a cover for me."

"Well, Swift must suspect something. That may be why he asked me about you."

"I'm afraid you may be right, and that's why I have to back

off at least for a while. I'll stay here the rest of the week and then take the kids back. But I still need someone here who can keep me up to speed on what Shiu and Swift are doing. I'm asking you to do it."

"Come on, Frank. This isn't my line of work. What happened with the governor was about ninety percent dumb luck. Hell, it was Swift who had the best nose for what was going on. Mostly I was just puzzled; he was suspicious.

"Besides, there's something about this that bothers me. Like 'em or not, I'm taking my wages from Shiu and Swift, and I'm not sure I want to be some kind of spy. I just don't think so."

Sanders shrugged. "Well, Bob, if you don't think this would be right, I ain't gonna lean on you. I gotta admit there's nothing solid to go on yet, but I surely do have a feeling that somewhere around here there's real rotten fish."

He looked up from his beer. "Anyway, can I depend on you not to talk about this?"

"For now, yes," I said. "But again, I'm not making any long-term promises."

"Best I can do, I guess," Sanders said, finishing his beer. "Shall we go back and rescue the kids?"

We walked back to the paper and found Frank's class clustered around one of the computer terminals on the city desk. A news story had been called up on the screen, and they were all intently scanning it.

"What have they got?" I asked Bill Grace.

"Cindy's budget hearing piece. The committee took testimony on the university appropriation, so they're interested."

The phone rang and Grace picked it up. He's an unflappable guy ordinarily, so I was surprised to see his eyes widen like a pair of sunnyside eggs in a skillet.

"Jesus, Dick, that sounds big. You go with them and I'll dig up somebody here to give you a hand," Grace said. He hung up and stood looking around the newsroom.

"What is it?" I asked.

"Christ, I don't know. Mooniman says the cops are mustering the whole day shift over at the jail and passing out rifles and riot guns. Listen, can you go over there right away to help out?"

"Sure," I said. I dug for a notebook in one of the desks and Grace said, "Damn it, I got no photographer. Whine's out shooting features."

A couple of the kids had turned away from the terminal and were listening. Sanders' daughter stepped up to Grace and said, "I'm a photographer. Have you got a camera I can use?"

"Oh, I don't know," Grace said. "This might be something hairy."

Sanders had come over. "She's a good photographer, Grace. And she knows how to take care of herself. She covered some dustups between right- and left-wing students at the college last year and did a damn good job."

Grace gave in quickly. "Bob, show her where the photo department is. Come on, Mooniman says whatever is happening is going down soon."

We grabbed a camera from Whine's cabinet and ran out to the street. About two blocks down, we saw what had to be every cop car in town heading our way. They pulled up at Kapplan Brothers' Department Store and the cops, wearing flak jackets and lugging enough hardware to invade Europe, piled out and began taking stations at the doors of the store and running around toward the rear. A couple of young guys in plainclothes I didn't recognize were waving them into place with hand signals and jabbering into walkie-talkies.

Liz and I ran down to the corner just as Mooniman got out of the chief's car which had brought up the rear of the cavalcade.

"Good God, Dick," I said, "what the hell is this?"

Mooniman looked grim. "They wouldn't tell me before we left, but I got it out of the chief on the way over. They've got some real hard case in the store. One of the Ten Most Wanted. The guys in suits are FBI from the city."

There was no more time to talk about it. On a hand signal from one of the federal agents, the cops rushed through the doors of the store. We cautiously approached, but were stopped on the sidewalk. "Stand back," a cop said. "There's liable to be shooting."

There wasn't any shooting, but within a minute there was the damndest screeching coming out of the store I've ever heard. It sounded like a cat with his tail caught in a door. Next, we heard glass breaking and men yelling and women screaming. We tried to peer in over the cop's shoulder, but whatever was happening was out of our line of sight.

"Hey, let us in," Mooniman told the cop. "The chief told me we could be in on this."

"He didn't tell me," the young cop said.

"He didn't tell you who he was gonna put on the midnight to six A.M. shift either," Mooniman said. "But I can give you a damn good guess if you screw up his chance to get good press on this story."

The cop hesitated, shrugged, and stood aside as the volume and variety of noise from inside increased. Dick led as we went into the main sales floor of the store.

Kapplan's was one of your old style department stores—a high-ceilinged, unpartitioned first floor with clusters of merchandise tables and display cases marking off the various departments. You could stand at the front and easily see all the way to the rear, where the elevators and dressing rooms were located. The departments on the first floor were all soft goods, men's and women's ready-to-wear, stationery, candy, and so on.

What we saw as we stepped into the store looked like an explosion in a laundry. Clothing of all descriptions was strewn in the aisles, display cases were tipped over and against the back wall, several knots of very frightened looking salespeople and customers were standing and crouching behind tables and clothing racks.

In the middle of the room about ten cops were gathered in

what looked like one of those rugby scrums, lurching and staggering as they struggled with someone we couldn't see.

But we could hear him. A stream of profanity like I've never heard, since my basic training sergeant stumbled into a slit trench, was coming out of the center of the heaving melee.

Liz jumped up on one of the tables, kicked aside a stack of polo shirts, and began taking pictures. I looked up and had one of those wondrous flashes of cognition that light up the mind like an aerial flare on a moonless night.

I had been instantly attracted to this pretty blonde girl when I first saw her, but that happened to me a lot. It was a function of the gonads with no reference to the brain. But now, as she stood on the table, oblivious to everything except the action and handling the camera like she had been born with it, I experienced the most complete and overwhelming feeling of warm joy of my life. If it wasn't something I'd eaten, it must have been love.

Mooniman and I tried to get closer, but the mass of struggling cops was moving toward the door. We had to stand aside as they went by and could see a man in the middle of the group being carried spread-eagle—a couple of cops on each arm and leg. He was bucking and squirming like a fresh-caught pickerel and screaming at the top of his lungs.

"Bastards! Sonsabitches! Dirty shits! Lemme down! Fuckin' cops, I'll kill you. Lemme down and I'll cream ya all! Lemme down, goddamn it!"

The man, bald except for a fringe of dirty gray hair around the side of his head, twisted around and sunk his teeth into the hand of one of the cops, whose turn it was to let out a bellow. He backed away and another cop tried to grab the man's arm, which flailed around and hit him square across the nose. Blood spurted and the man lunged at the cop's leg with his mouth. As he bit down, another policeman pulled his billy club out of his belt and whacked the man across the side of the head with a sound like a baseball bat against a

watermelon. The man sagged, but as the cops tried again to
lift him, he got a leg loose and fetched one of the officers a
kick just below the belt buckle. The cop with the club really
wound up this time and skulled the guy hard enough to roll
his eyes back into his head. Peace was restored.

The cops dragged the guy outside and laid him out on the
sidewalk. The man couldn't have been taller than five feet
three nor weighed more than 120 pounds. He wore a baggy
coverall with "Kapplan Bros." on the sleeve and the name
"Norris" above the chest pocket, and appeared to be about
fifty, maybe fifty-five years old, with a seamed face, baggy
eyes, and a nose that had been broken several times. He
looked like a punched-out lightweight or maybe a jockey
who had gotten trampled a couple of times.

He came to a lot faster than anyone hit that hard had a
right to. With difficulty and more shrieking, the cops
shackled his legs and cuffed his hands behind his back. Then
they stood him up and began propelling him toward one of
the cars.

"Did you see that, Bob? The guy couldn't have been bigger than Mickey Rooney," Mooniman said as the squad car
pulled away. "But did you ever see such a fighter?"

Mooniman and I hitched a ride in another squad car to the
jail and Liz headed back to the paper with the camera.

Gib Bock, the chief, called us into his office. With him
was one of the FBI men.

"Gentlemen," Gib said, "we have just taken into custody
Norris Barkis, one of the ten most-wanted criminals in the
United States. This man is one of the most vicious felons in
the country, and I can tell you that it is to the credit of this
department that . . ."

The agent interrupted. "Just a moment, chief. I am Calvin
Decker, Special Agent in Charge in the City. Mr. Barkis is a
federal prisoner, and any information about this apprehen-
sion will have to be released by the Bureau."

"Now, wait a minute," Bock said.

"Chief, the Bureau is very grateful to you and your men for their help. But the information function is outside your jurisdiction."

"The hell you say, mister," Bock retorted. "My guys made the collar, my guys got chewed up, and I'm gonna tell the press about it. Don't give me that federal jurisdiction crap."

The agent stared at him and shrugged. You could just tell he was thinking, "OK, you old fart. Lucky for you J. Edgar ain't around any more."

"Okay," Gib said. "This Barkis is a fugitive from the federal pen downstate in Illinois. He was doing twenty to thirty for a string of robberies and assaults as long as a horse pecker. He made the most-wanted list two months ago. He's been working at Kapplan's for six weeks as a stock clerk and used the name Norris Harkin. Mostly he worked in the stockrooms, but once in a while he had to bring stuff out to the sales floor. Well, one of the old ladies who shop at Kapplan's recognized him day before yesterday from a mug shot in one of those true detective magazines. Called us and we notified the FBI."

Bock threw a glance at the agent. "As a courtesy to them, we waited till they got up here this morning and busted the guy. Jumped him while he was stacking ladies' undies."

"Was he armed?" Mooniman asked. "I know damn well he resisted."

"No gun," Gib said. "But he used his usual weapon."

"What's that?" I asked.

"His goddamn teeth," the chief said. "The guy is a street fighter . . . goes for ears, fingers, noses, you name it, he'll bite it. He took chunks out of three of our guys before we got him down. They're over at City General getting tetanus and God knows what other shots. We're going to slap mayhem charges on him to go with the rest."

"Can we interview him?" Mooniman asked.

"Wait a minute," the agent started. The chief glared at him.

"Not now, Dick. He's back there in the cell block still raving and acting the nut. We got to book him and all the rest first. We'll consider it when things cool down a bit." Bock made it sound final, and knowing his man, Dick didn't argue.

Mooniman and I left, driving back to the paper in his car. Swift was at the city desk with Grace.

"All right, Mooniman, get cracking. Claggett is phoning Washington for more details on this bloke, and he'll give you notes. You start writing and don't spare the color. Put some pepper in it, old boy."

Swift told me to get Liz's pictures, which were drying in the darkroom, and write some captions. "We're going to take the whole front page for this. The girl's pictures are damn good, so we're going to run them big, but keep the captions simple."

Everybody went to work and Swift hopped from Moon-iman to Grace to Claggett to me, prodding us to hurry. When he found out about the little old lady who fingered Barkis, he sent Judy Teach and Liz out to interview her.

(Whine came back in the midst of all the activity to learn he had missed the best local story in years, while he was out photographing a cooking class. "Tandee's luck," he said. "I'll be out shooting a wedding when a plane crashes into the Capitol dome.")

Finally, the story went into the computer and the photos were sent off to the camera room. Swift sat down to lay out the front page and compose the headlines.

It was the first time I had seen him in action. The layout didn't take long as he swiftly blocked out the space for the photos, the headlines, and the copy. Then he slumped at the desk staring vacantly at Grace. He pawed at the printout of the copy, chewed on a copy pencil, and then suddenly sat bolt upright with a wicked grin on his face.

He began scribbling large block letters on a sheet of copy paper. Finished in minutes, he handed the paper to Grace and said, "This is the banner. Seventy-two point. The rest is forty-eight point, decked below the big one. Get them going in the shop."

I just got a glance at the sheet. It said:

COPS NAB CANNIBAL DESPERADO

NORRIS 'THE BITER' BARKIS CAPTURED IN LOCAL STORE

'MOST WANTED' FUGITIVE SINKS TEETH INTO THREE OFFICERS

Swift turned to Mooniman. "Now, get your arse back to the jail and tell that tinhorn chief we demand to see the prisoner. I want an interview."

Mooniman started to get up. Swift reached out and took his arm. "Oh, and take this new kid Bright with you. I want him to see how a good reporter works."

Mooniman smiled and waved at Kirk Bright, a young reporter who had just started with the paper that week. They left together.

Mooniman told me later what happened when they got to the jail. Gib told them that Barkis was still raising hell and wouldn't let anyone get near his cell without beginning to shriek and curse. Mooniman finally talked the chief into at least letting him and Bright take a look at Barkis to see if he'd talk to them.

Barkis went into a fit when the chief walked into the cell block and screamed obscenities at Mooniman. But when he saw young Bright, Barkis suddenly quieted down, looking almost scared. Mooniman asked if they could talk to him and Barkis—acting like a lamb who has just been asked to dance by the wolf—agreed with no argument.

"I'll talk to him," he said, nodding at Bright. Mooniman said he didn't know what had happened, but he wasn't going to push it. He let the cub ask the questions.

The interview was a dandy. Barkis acknowledged he was the man the cops had been looking for, but when young Bright asked him about his penchant for chomping hunks of meat out of people he took a dislike to, the little guy got indignant.

"Listen, I ain't no bruiser and where I grew up a kid had to use whatever he had. So I used my teeth. I found out a long time ago a good chomp and a growl makes the biggest bastards back off. But this business about me tearing meat out of people all the time is a lot of crap the cops put out to make themselves look like they captured some kind of wild man from Borneo or something."

Barkis got an injured look on his face.

"I may bite, damn it, but I never swallow."

Swift held the paper to get the interview in. He gave Mooniman the main story byline and put Bright's name on the interview.

After the paper was in, the usual crowd repaired to the Next Door to hash over the story. Kirk Bright had gone over earlier to celebrate his first byline and came over to buy us a round when we arrived.

Bright was sitting with us, his back to the door, when Sanders arrived. I introduced him around and when Bright turned to shake hands, Sanders started like he had been poked with a stick.

Sanders put his hand on my shoulder. "Bob, can I speak with you for a moment?"

We stepped over to the bar and Sanders whispered, "That kid. Where'd he come from?"

"A new boy," I said. "I think I heard somebody say he was an Ivy Leaguer come to make his way in the gritty world of small town newspapering. He did pretty well his first time out of the box, I hear." I told him what Mooniman had said about the interview.

"Jesus," Sanders said. "Listen, you-all got back issues over at the paper?" When I said we did, Sanders pulled me out of the bar and back to the *CR&P*.

In the dusty file room on the third floor, he said, "Find 1957. November." I rooted in the stacks and found the month he wanted.

Sanders flipped the yellowing pages and finally came to what he wanted.

"Here," he said, "look at this."

On the front page of the paper was a large group photograph of half a dozen men of varying ages standing on a road in some kind of country setting. The paper was a little yellowed around the edges, but the bound volume hadn't been handled much and the print and the photograph was still clear.

Sanders pointed at a young, good-looking man with thick dark hair who was the spitting image of Kirk Bright.

"That picture was taken by the New York state police when they rousted the mob at the Appalachian meeting in 1957. The crime summit, we called it."

"Who's the guy that looks like Bright?"

"The midwestern delegate, a young but up-and-coming button man named Clean Gene Bright. A very mean hombre in those days.

"It doesn't surprise me that Barkis got cooperative when he saw the kid. After the knocking around he took, he probably thought at first he was looking at the father. And nobody in his line of work ever gave Clean Gene an argument."

Sanders closed the big book.

"Lookee here, Bob. I told you I didn't really have anything solid to go on, and I still don't. We don't even know for sure this kid is Gene Bright's son. It's purely circumstantial, but it'd be the damn coincidence of the century if he ain't kin to Gene. That's something I think I can check. And even if he is related, it's also circumstantial. But this is a fact: When the mob goes into some new venture, straight or crooked, they almost always have someone on the spot to keep an eye on the investment."

Sanders looked thoughtful. "There's another possibility, too. A lot of the older guys don't want their kids in the rackets. They send them to college to be doctors, lawyers, business majors . . . maybe newspaper men. This young fellow might not know if his father is involved in the paper, even if his old man smoothed the way for him to get the job. I don't know, but I sure as hell am going to try to find out . . . and I sure as hell wish you could see your way clear to help."

I didn't really need the sales talk. The resemblance between young Kirk Bright and the man in the twenty-five-year-old photograph had made up my mind for me.

"I'm in, Frank."

CHAPTER 9

Frank and his kids finished a week of observing the *Capital Register & Press* and headed back to the university—minus one of their number. Swift may have been suspicious of Sanders, but he either didn't make the connection between Frank and Liz or didn't think she would be a problem. He definitely liked the work she did on the Barkis story—enough to offer her a job as Whine's assistant.

Liz was hesitant.

"Oh, Mr. Swift, there's nothing I'd rather do more, but I've still got a semester to go at school. Can I come back when I've finished?"

Swift fluffed his beard. "Young woman, do you know how many jobs there are in daily journalism in this country? About five thousand, and I'm told there are fifty thousand journalism students in the United States. You're a talented youngster, but I'm sure there are others just as gifted who would jump at this opportunity. I'm offering it to you now, but I can't hold the place. It may be filled when you get that precious diploma."

Frank, standing behind Swift, was listening to all this and when Liz looked helplessly at him responded with a wink. She smiled and said, "Mr. Swift, you've got yourself a photographer."

"A photographer's assistant, young woman. You did an excellent job in a dicey situation, but don't get the idea you've mastered your craft. You've got an apprenticeship to serve, and it isn't going to be as exciting as your first taste of the job. But with Mr. Tandee's help, we can make you into a photographer."

Liz looked down at her shoes, appropriately chastened. Swift told her to report to Tandee, who already had been informed he might be getting an assistant. Whine had been complaining for years that the paper needed a second shooter, but of course his reaction, expressed over a beer at the Next Door, was, "Hell. Now I got to play teacher for some young broad that got lucky. And I suppose she'll be rubbing up against Swift and Grace to get the good jobs."

As it turned out, Liz was well aware that she had a lot to learn and quickly established a relationship with Whine that made clear she was willing to do the donkey work in the lab if he would give her the pointers she needed to master the camera work. In a week, Whine was worrying aloud about how he'd be able to get Liz on the payroll as a regular photographer after he broke her in on the job.

I had a drink with Frank before he left. He gave me several telephone numbers where I could reach him at the university and suggested that I compare notes with Liz on anything I turned up.

"She knows what you're looking for?"

"A sharp young lady, Bob. She figured out before we came here that I was interested in something besides the way this sheet is produced. I told her months ago that we were going to do the short course between semesters in the city, and when I switched signals she guessed that I had one of my little sideline jobs. Yep, she knows, and if I'd had any idea she would be staying here, I wouldn't have had to bring you into this."

I must have looked a little offended, because he reached over the table and tapped my arm. "Now don't get your back up, Bob. She isn't in a position to see and hear what you can and the way it works out, I've got twice as many eyes and ears here than I expected. But do keep in touch with her. If anyone gets nosey, it'll look more natural if she's contacting me regularly than if you are."

Jesus. It was obvious that Swift wasn't the only semi-paranoid I was dealing with.

But it was surprising how soon I had something to pass on to Frank, and how quickly I found myself playing cloak and dagger.

About a week later, I was leaving a senate budget hearing during a recess when Ed Ridgely, the state commerce commissioner, beckoned me over to his seat in the back of the committee room. Next to him was a tall, gray-haired man I had seen before but couldn't place.

"Sit down if you're not in a hurry, Bob," Ridgely said. "You know Marty Gonsalves here?"

I leaned across and shook the man's hand. "I should, but . . ."

"He's the manager of Capital International. You've probably seen him out there."

"Oh sure," I said. "I covered a news conference you had when the airport expansion bill was before the legislature."

"Marty tells me the paper is getting into air transport. What's it all about?"

I remembered the stuff in the incorporation papers about transportation, but couldn't imagine that was what he was talking about.

"Search me, Ed. What do you mean 'getting into air transport'?"

"Marty says the paper has bought a helicopter and is renting hangar space at his place. You don't know about it?"

"Hell, Ed, the owners must have forgotten to clear it with me. Maybe we're gonna be using it to flit around the state covering stories."

"Not in this sucker," Gonsalves said.

"No?"

"Not likely. The helicopter you all are getting is for toting a hell of a lot heavier loads than reporters. It's a Sikorsky

CH54A. . . . one of those humungous big machines the army uses to hoist big stuff, like bridge trusses and trucks. Some lumber and construction companies have 'em, too. Funny-lookin' things—about seventy feet long, nose to tail, and skinny—look like grasshoppers, but they call 'em Sky-cranes."

"First damn thing I heard about it, Marty. Is it already out at the airport?"

Gonsalves obviously felt set up to be telling a reporter something about his own business. "It was ferried in day before yesterday. They're fitting it out now for your pilot."

"Our pilot?"

"Sure, that little fellow, the Jap, or whatever he is. They're putting in a new seat and modifying the controls so he can reach 'em. I tell you, I never would have spotted the runty little guy for a chopper jockey, but he showed me his license. He's checked out in just about anything you can get to leave the ground."

"You're talking about Shiu? Shigetsu Shiu?"

"That's what it says on his ticket. He didn't have a lot to say, but I take it he learned to fly copters in Laos or Vietnam or one of those damn places. When he came in, I said that was a lot of aircraft to handle, and he got a little puffed up and said it ain't hard at all if people ain't shooting at you, like where he first started flying."

I thought about that all afternoon and decided I ought to pass it on to Sanders. I went by the paper after work, but Liz wasn't in the photo lab, so I tried the Next Door. The regulars were in the usual booth and Liz was sitting down the row with some of the younger staff members. Kirk Bright was there and an older guy, a hulk in a tight sports jacket, was sitting next to him. I'd never seen him around, but the paper was hiring a lot of new people.

I had a beer with the regulars and when Liz got up and headed for the ladies', I patted my pocket and said I was out of cigarettes. I went to the bar, asked for change, and chatted with the bartender until I spotted Liz coming out. Then I walked back to the cigarette machine and met her in the aisle.

"Need to talk," I said in what I hoped was a mutter. "Half an hour in the Clark bar?" She smiled and nodded and went back to her friends.

I finished my beer, excused myself and left by the rear door, the closest route to the paper's parking lot, and the way out most of the staff used when they headed home. I walked down the alley, around the block and into the side door of the Clark Hotel, across the street from the Next Door.

The bar was small and dark and I sat at one of those tables the size of a Susan B. Anthony dollar near the door. Liz showed up in about forty minutes and looked into the gloom. I stood up and touched her arm.

"Here."

"Oh, hi, Bob. Sorry it took me so long, but I wanted to hear what Kirk was talking about. Swift has given him a special assignment, and it sounds to me like it's going to be something."

"Now what?" I asked.

"Swift wants an exposé of the massage parlors off Capitol Circle. He says this town has a red-light district operating as wide open as Times Square, and nobody seems to be paying attention. He picked Kirk 'cause he's new in town and he wants him to do some first-person pieces about what goes on in The Three Bares and the Fugue U Ranch." Liz giggled.

"Oh, God," I said. "Another anti-vice crusade. You know what'll happen? The members of the city council and the legislature will denounce such goings-on in the fair capital of the state, and then trample each other to get to those joints to make sure they don't have any credit card charge slips being held for payment."

The waitress came to our so-called table. Liz ordered an ale and I took a beer.

"Listen," I said. "I've got something your dad might be able to use." I told her about the helicopter and Shiu's plans to pilot it.

"Wow, that is strange stuff. And I saw something yesterday that may have something to do with it. Rick sent me over to the company garage to get the photographer's car greased, and I noticed the circulation trucks were all parked on the street. The big fenced-in yard they have there is filled with huge boxes."

"Boxes?"

"Well, containers. Big—maybe the size of truck bodies."

I thought about that, and after we'd had a couple of beers, we left the Clark—got a couple of nice leers from some lobbyists I knew as we went through the lobby—picked up my car and drove to the building by the river where the paper serviced and parked its dozen or so delivery vans.

I drove up to the compound and looked inside. There were six metal containers about the size of beer truck boxes along the fence. They had small metal wheels—like the garbage dumpsters you see outside office buildings—and something Liz hadn't mentioned, a good-sized tractor with a towing hitch on the back. Walking alongside the fence, I paced off the open space in the compound . . . at least 150 feet. There was room enough for Shiggy's copter.

"I think you're right. I bet those containers have something to do with the chopper. You better phone Frank tonight."

Liz looked at me. "There's a problem, Bob. I'm sharing a place with a girl I knew in school last year, and it really is too small for private phone conversations if she's home."

I swear my heart was pure when I suggested we'd have to make the call from my place. That's where we went and made the call, and ordered pizza, and talked into the night, and went to bed.

Liz usually dressed in jeans and sweaters that were large enough to do very little for her figure, but I found her to be very much a full-grown woman. She also acted much more like one than the coeds I remembered from a few—well, maybe more than a few—years back on campus.

At some point I believe I said something about being old enough to be her father, which caused her to raise up on her elbow and declare, well, she liked her father, but inasmuch as she had never even been tempted to try incest, she was altogether more content with the present arrangement.

"Christ, I wonder what he'd do if he knew I took you home and bundled you into bed," I said.

Liz laughed. "Seduced his innocent daughter? Bob, I was living off campus with a guy for more than a year. Daddy didn't like him much, and I wouldn't be surprised if he would be relieved if he knew I was with a man who didn't think the Rolling Stones were the flower of civilization and that an evening without an hour on a bong was wasted forever."

"What do you think?"

"I think you are a nice, funny, gentle man—a lot better in the sack than I would have guessed—a lot more interested in how it's going for me than some I've known. Now I'm going to sleep unless you're going to throw me out."

"Oh, God no," I said—and slept the sleep of the happily spent.

It was most of a week before Kirk Bright's project developed. I had finished a long feature I was doing on the speaker and called Grace to ask when I should figure it would be run.

"Sure as shit not tomorrow, Bob. Swift is taking the front page and two inside for Bright's whorehouse pieces. Claggett is reading them with Swift leaning over his shoulder, and every time he goes to cut something, Old Whiskers jumps on his ass. Drew told him a while ago that something in one of the pieces was too raw for our town's readers, and you know what Swift said? 'I'm not putting out this paper for this piss-ant town.'"

The next day's *CR&P* was a sight to behold. The front page had a big picture of the block with most of the town's massage parlors and shots of the girls through the front windows and standing in the open doorways. I especially liked the one of the lady wearing a Girl Scout uniform with the blouse opened to the navel and the skirt ending closer to the crotch than the knees.

The headlines had Swift's unerring touch:

SODOM IN CAPITOL'S SHADOW!
HOOKERS PLY WARES IN
BOGUS HEALTH CLUBS

POLICE TURN BLIND EYE
TO LOCAL DENS OF VICE

DO MASSAGE PARLORS FOSTER
HERPES, VD, AND AIDS?
ARE TEEN GIRLS RECRUITED
FOR LIVES OF SHAME?

The stories convinced me that Sanders probably was wrong about young Bright being an overseer for the mob at the paper. Maybe his papa was major motion in the Mafia, but Bright wrote about sex-for-sale like a country parson's kid. The headlines were pure Granville Swift, but the text was more like Tom Swift.

At one point, Bright wrote of the customer (who but himself?) who went into a massage parlor and asked if he could receive treatment to ease the discomfort of a charley horse.

> The scantily clad young woman, who could not have been much older than eighteen, laughed heartily at the request. "We play some horsey here, Charley, but that ain't my specialty. Maybe you'd like a little leather workover?"

The customer asked what that would involve and the girl came over and wrapped her arms around him. "Fun, honey, fun. But if you don't go that route, I can play it just as straight as the missionary called for. Now, are you going to be cash or credit card?"

It was obvious from this exchange that something more than conventional physical therapy was being dispensed at this establishment which, in fact, appeared to be too dimly lit and too gaudily decorated to be an authentic clinic.

The customer hesitated and the young woman said, "Look, if you would rather see one of the other girls, I'll send one out. Why don't I show you one of our rooms and have someone else talk to you?"

She took the customer by the hand and led him to a small room almost completely filled with a round bed. "This is our deluxe suite," she said. "Sit down and relax and someone will be with you in a minute."

The room was semidarkened, but after a few minutes the customer was able to see. There was one chair in a corner with several towels draped over the back. On a shelf was a bottle of baby oil and a can of talcum powder. The walls of the room were covered with a red, flocked wallpaper. Four or five unframed centerfold photographs of frontally nude women were tacked to the walls.

After about five minutes, a tall blonde woman wearing a negligee came into the room. Without a word, she let slip the shoulder strap on one side of the garment and exposed a large breast. This she lifted in her hand and thrust toward the customer. "You want a sample?"

The customer hurriedly excused himself, saying he had left home without his wallet, and left. As the door closed behind him, he heard the blonde woman say to someone inside, "Hell, it wasn't money that one didn't have in his pants."

At the Next Door that night, the Bright stories were the talk of the place, and when the kid came in about 10 P.M.

with the heavyweight type I had seen the previous week, he became the center of attention.

Shep Carley, I was sorry but not surprised to see, was in that sodden state that follows drunken liveliness and precedes "flat on his face." Shep was no barroom bravo, but he got nasty after enough beer, and this night it was Kirk Bright who was the target.

"Hey, kid, how much of the paper's money did you blow in those whorehouses?" Shep paused and giggled. "You get that, Bob? How much did he blow?"

Bright looked up from the booth he was in. "Oh, I didn't actually spend any of the paper's money on the story, Mr. Carley."

"Oh, you paid your own dough? Was the nooky that good?"

Bright looked distinctly uncomfortable. "No, no. I didn't spend any money at all. I didn't, ah, go all the way at any of those places."

"Come on, kid. You had a chance to get your ashes hauled on Swift's dollar and you passed? What are you, queer?"

Suddenly Shep found himself lifted about eight inches off the floor and staring Bright's bruiser friend in the face.

"Mr. Bright says he didn't spend any money at them places. That don't make him no faggot, understand?" He let go and Shep dropped, falling to his knees.

"Hey," the big man said, looking down at Carley. "Maybe you're the queer, huh?" He pushed Shep and toppled him on his side, where he remained.

Bright got out of the booth and motioned the bruiser away. "Kenny, cut it out. He was just kidding."

Bright helped one of the other young reporters lift Shep into a seat. He took the big man over to a corner and spoke quietly but with emphasis. Then he went over to Shep and leaned down. "Hey, I'm sorry, Mr. Carley. My roommate just got a little excited. Let me buy you a beer."

Carley was so soused he apparently thought he had fallen

by himself. He smiled at Bright and nodded. The big man came back to the booth and stuck out his hand.

"Hey, I'm sorry, buddy. I thought you was giving Kirk a hard time, and I figgered a guy has to stand up for his roommie."

"Mr. Carley, this is Kenny Kehler, my roommate," Bright said, looking around the group as if an explanation had been demanded. "We've been friends since I was a kid, and when I got this job I found out he was working here and had an apartment big enough for two. So, with first-year pay being what it is, I moved in with him."

Shep nodded in a bewildered way and entered phase three of his usual drinking progression. He passed out.

We were just getting ready to hoist Carley out of the booth and start pumping some coffee into him when Dick Mooniman came in.

"Jesus, what a night," he said as he signaled for a beer.

"What now?" Claggett asked.

"I been running since eight o'clock. The whorehouse stories got the cops off their asses and they hit all the massage joints. There's enough women in kimonos down at the lockup to cast a Japanese opera."

He took a pull out of the bottle. "And something else. About a dozen pissed-off customers got pulled in with the girls, including, for Christ's sake, both the present and immediate past publishers of that pillar of community morals, the *Capital Register & Press*."

"Shiu?"

"Morgan?"

"Both, literally in the flesh, the cops said. They were having a little foursome at the Three Bares when the doors came down. By the time they got to the cop house, one of them got through to Swift, and he was there with bail when they arrived wrapped in sheets."

"So what happened?" I asked.

"Well, I came back to the paper and started writing the

story. I didn't know what we were going to do about Shiu and Morgan, but I thought sure we'd give a good splash to the raids."

"And?"

"Swift came back madder than a bear that got waked up by a New Year's party. I asked him how much we wanted on the story, and he picked a phone book off the desk and flung it clear across the room.

"'A brief,' he said. 'Just write a straight piece saying the police raided the health clubs and arrested a dozen or whatever it was number of women. That's all.'

"I asked him if we shouldn't say the raids followed our exposé, and he looked at me like he wanted to cry. 'Just a brief. Bloody policy. We'd be doing it up brown—I can tell you, if I had my way—but we've got a publisher who doesn't read his own paper and didn't even know we had blown the whistle on his favorite relaxation. Bloody idiot! I don't care if he fucks everything that moves, but now he's ruined the best story around this dreary place in weeks. I bloody well won't forget this.'

"He stamped into his office and here I am—finished work a lot sooner than I expected."

Kirk Bright had been listening to this with his mouth open. "I don't understand, Mr. Mooniman. Does this mean we won't be following up on my stories?"

Mooniman took a gulp of beer. "It means, kid, what Joe Liebling or somebody said about freedom of the press. It belongs to them that owns one."

CHAPTER 10

"The primary is coming," Swift said.

I stood in his office—the chairs were buried under papers, books, and what looked like pizza boxes and hamburger cartons of condemnable age and condition—and wondered what the managing editor had on his mind now. One thing I knew—he didn't call me over from the statehouse to tell me something he knew I knew.

"I know. I wrote you a memo—about covering the campaign this year."

Swift poked around in a pile of papers on his desk and with two fingers gingerly extracted my note from between a used paper napkin and a Mighty Mac wrapper.

"You call this a coverage plan? You want to spend a couple of days with each of the candidates and come back and write an . . . overview? An overview, for God's sake? What about daily coverage?"

"Well, we've always used the wires for that. Fargo said it was silly to send people out to duplicate what we already were paying them for. And besides, these campaigns charge 150 percent of first class airfare to travel with them. He said Morgan would have a kitten if we spent that kind of money."

"Bugger Morgan . . . and Barton too! We've got national figures coming into this state for a week, maybe more, and we're going to give them grown-up newspaper coverage. I want a plan to make some of these twits that have been sneering at us sit up and take notice.

"I don't imagine we've got any budding Theodore Whites around here, Wartovsky, but see if you can find at least three reporters on this staff who know the difference between a Democrat and a doorstop. And start making arrangments for our people to cover these candidates when they start, what is it? . . . stamping in this state."

Another surprise. I'd been at the *CR&P* in two presidential years, and it seemed to me the management always tried to pretend the campaign was taking place in Patagonia, even when our primary was getting top billing in the Eastern papers and on the networks. Now Swift was calling for respectable coverage of a political story that might not have a spot of blood or whiff of sex. Amazing.

Our presidential primary used to be one of the big shows every four years. It was our voters who sent Wendell Willkie back to Wall Street in 1944 and showed that Jack Kennedy could win in the Midwest in 1960, but since then we'd pretty much been upstaged by the likes of Iowa, Illinois, and even Nebraska, for God's sake.

Four years earlier, none of the candidates made big efforts in our state. That may have been connected with the fact that the incumbent vice president was from the neighboring state and passed the word to party leaders that if any of them started playing footsie with the guy who was challenging the president, he would personally see to it that our next interstate highway project went directly through the state Capitol grounds.

In the other party, the old actor tied up our delegates in a hurry when he reminded everyone that he once had made a movie that glorified the state's greatest football coach. Of such monumental factors are the hard-headed decisions of big time politics made.

This year, there was a faint chance we might get some action again. Nuclear power and arms control were emerging as big medicine in the national campaign, and we'd already had some epic referendum fights on both. (Our voters relished advising the president, the Congress, the United Nations, and the Soviet Union on how to run the world, but it was a root canal job to get them to approve a bond issue to repair their own highways.)

Anyway, *The New York Times* announced early on that we would be "a crucial testing ground" in the primaries because of our "prairie populist" resistance to such Eastern notions as atomic power and city-flattening missiles.

Not to be outanalyzed, *The Washington Post* proclaimed that we knew nothing about nukes, but that there would be a "key confrontation" in our state on the issue of dairy price supports.

It also had a ten-thousand-word profile of a guy who had walked away from a job as a New York advertising copy writer to run a dairy farm in our state. He obviously had gone from one job to another to shovel manure.

The lady who did the piece obviously hadn't spent much time on farms. One of the "anecdotes" in the piece told how she thought only male animals grew horns and was surprised to find that cows, "the female of the species," come fully equipped in that department. Lent some depth to the piece I thought.

Then, just when we thought we knew what we were concerned about in our state, the *Los Angeles Times* weighed in with the declaration that our voters really were apathetic about the issues and the battle would really be one of media consultants and direct mail fund-raising skills.

With the stakes so clearly stated, ABC unveiled plans for a six-week series of tracking polls that would place a network researcher with a portable video camera and recorder in each of 467 typical homes to record the ebb and flow of opinion as it took place around the dining room tables of the state.

CBS flew an antinuclear activist, a dairy farmer, and a professional campaign consultant to New York to be interviewed by Diane Sawyer, and NBC responded by sending Jane

Pauley to have breakfast on a farm whose owner said he, for one, would be proud to have an MX missile in the south forty if it would help "keep the durn commynists in Roosha where they belonged."

It was my private suspicion that the real attraction of our state to the national political press was the quality of the German restaurants in the city, where most of the campaigns headquartered. But who was I to question my betters?

So I scribbled out a news coverage plan for Swift and left it in his mailbox. The next day, I got another summons to his fishbowl office.

"This is somewhat better. But we're going to add something. We need stories by someone who sees this state with a fresh eye. Someone who doesn't think it's perfectly normal when a candidate for president of the United States steps in a cow turd," Swift said with a meaningful look.

He handed me a book. "You know of this fellow?"

I needed only a glance. The book was that classic, *Lust, Trust and Bust,* Naughton Newton's abstract impressionistic tour de force on the 1980 campaign. It had a half chapter about our state's political climate, and so far as I could tell, it must have been written after a careful examination of the situation in California. It was entertaining enough, but the discussion of citrus ranching and alpine ski resorts as the lynchpins of our economy was somewhat distracting.

One of the national political reporters I met during that campaign came through town shortly after Newton's book was published in 1981, and I asked him where the hell the guy got his information.

"Oh, Christ, don't tell me you people take Knocko Newton's stuff seriously? Where does he get his information? Right off the west wall, that's where. Shit, Knocko was in Boston during most of the 1980 campaign. He was on his way to cover New Hampshire in February when he ran into this half-Latvian, half-Osage Indian girl in the bar of the Winthrop Plaza. He moved in till June with her and her father, an old drunk who sits around wrapped in a blanket and a feather in his hair and puts away a fifth of sloe gin every afternoon. Knocko loved 'em both. He said the broad had a tongue that should have been awarded an MIT Ph.D., and claimed old Here's-Looking-at-You-Kid could slice open a fresh-caught mackerel and give you a better reading on the next primary from its insides than Harris or Gallup could get from a week of polling. And lemme tell you, there were a couple times that year he was a lot closer than I was."

Remembering that, I looked up from the book and started to object. "This guy is a phony. . . ."

"Phony!" Swift roared. "That book contains some of the best writing about politics I have read in thirty years. Most of these campaign books read like they were written by a spinster school marm. Newton may not be one of your deep political philosophers, but at least he recognizes that these politicians you get so excited about are just as susceptible to human failings as any undereducated, oversexed film star. I just wish I could get you and some of the other nancies I inherited on this staff to write like Newton."

Swift paused, taking the book back from me. "Besides, if he's a phony, how do you explain the fact that the book was twenty-eight weeks on the bestseller list?"

How could you argue with logic like that? I opened my mouth to try, but Swift raised his hand.

"I called you here to tell you that we've signed Newton to do two weeks of exclusive primary coverage for us. I want you to fit him into the coverage and assign one of our people to help him with the logistics—transport, reservations, and so on."

"Christ! He's got to have a wet nurse, too?"

"Just do it, bucko. We're paying a good piece of change for this, and I want to see some writing like he did in this book."

We didn't see Newton right away. The candidates—the skinny senator with all the hair, the young governor who married the movie star, and the old general who wanted to prove he could do the job better if somebody would just put him in charge—all made forays into the state as the primary pace picked up in the East and the South, and we did a credible job of covering them without Knocko's help.

One sunny afternoon, Liz and I were at the airport waiting for the governor's charter to arrive when she poked me in the arm and pointed to a hangar about a quarter mile away. A small tractor was pulling the oddest-looking aircraft I had ever seen out of the building, and behind it came strutting none other than the eminent publisher of the *Capital Register & Press*.

Shiu, looking like a Smurf in a space suit next to the huge silver-painted helicopter, clambered up into the cockpit and in a few minutes the gigantic rotors began swinging slowly. After a period of running up the engines, the ungainly machine moved out onto the field and slowly rose into the air. It went up a couple of hundred feet and headed toward town with a great clatter.

The governor's plane landed a few minutes later and we went to work. Liz observed as we followed him around town the rest of the day that he looked passable and sounded plausible, but it must have been something he kept behind a zipper that attracted the famous movie beauty who married him. "He might talk a woman to sleep, but not to bed," she commented.

Liz still was spending most of her time in the photo lab at the paper, but she was getting more frequent assignments to take pictures. Whine's initial suspicion of her had given way to a kind of teacher's pride in an apt pupil, and he was giving her jobs that ordinarily he would have jumped to take himself. I was amazed one afternoon to hear him arguing with Hank Terry about sending Liz to cover a basketball game.

"Don't be such a chauvinist pig, Hank," Whine was saying. "The camera can't tell whether its button is being pushed by a guy or a gal, and this one is a natural photographer. I'm getting tired of spending three nights a week watching a bunch of pimply freaks bounce a ball around, and I know damn well Liz will do a good job."

Liz also was spending more and more time at my place. She kept her clothes at the apartment she shared with her girlfriend, but more nights than not she bedded down at my place. A little bit at a time, we talked about me—the failed marriage, the fun and games that followed, and the casual and occasional relationships that gradually became the rule after the first flush of freedom.

"Do you want to get married again?" she asked.

"God, no. Once bitten and all that . . ."

"Well, you may change your mind. I better tell you, I'm definitely not planning to get married at least until I'm thirty. I'm happy now and I hope we can continue to enjoy each other, but if my staying here nights and all is going to complicate things, we better bag the arrangement. You're the best thing that's come along for me yet, but I'm not even thinking about anything permanent."

I guess I sulked a bit after that until I realized I was involved in a role reversal. I was the girl whose fellow wanted to sleep with her but not "get serious." So I just relaxed and enjoyed.

On the night of the governor's visit, we were having a few late ones at the Next Door and talking about Shiu and the helicopter.

Grace, who like everyone else at the paper had heard about the helicopter and had no more idea than anyone else what its purpose was, said the city desk had received three angry phone calls from an old lady who lived near the paper's circulation garage. She complained that a noisy flying machine had been landing and taking off for an hour, and if it didn't stop there was going to be trouble.

"Said she'd take a shotgun to it if it kept scaring her cats," Grace said. "I switched the call up to Shiu's office."

Liz and I phoned Frank that night with a progress report, but it turned out he had more news for us.

"This is beginning to form a picture. The Center had some people do some checkin' around the city and over at Chicago, and they picked up rumors that somebody apparently is planning to move into those big bedroom suburbs with a new daily paper. They couldn't find out who, 'cept that there seemed to be some big money behind them. Conglomerate money one report says. I think Swift and Shiu are connected, but I've gotta do some more snooping. What I need are some documents that pin this down.

"Oh, and a guy I know in Washington did some checking on your flying publisher. It may boggle the mind, but it turns out that this Shigetsu Shiu was one of the legendary soldiers of fortune of Indochina. He flew light planes and helicopters, probably for the CIA, in Laos, Cambodia, and 'Nam. Came to the states when the show folded over there. Some talk about him flying in the north-south drug trade. No arrests, but they were watchin' him 'till he came out here.

"He also has quite a personal background. His mother was the secretary of a Japanese military governor in China; his father was a Chinese janitor at the headquarters in Shanghai. When it got impossible for them to disguise the fact that they had been engaging in some verboten Sino-Japanese fraternization, they took off for the hills and finally settled in Saigon. The kid took to hanging around the airport, got a job as a mechanic's helper, and somebody taught him to fly. Turned out he had a real flair for it, but because he was so small he never could get a regular airline job. Wound up flyin' for whoever would pay, and before the Americans arrived was managing a charter service.

"My guy says Shiu also fancies himself as a premier lady's man. Had a string of gals all over Asia, but favored tall, blonde, English-type ladies. He had to leave Hong Kong in a hurry when he took a shine to the wife of an attaché at the British embassy and made the mistake of tryin' to crawl in her bedroom window one night. Her hubby collared him and told the cops he thought he had captured a large monkey until he got the lights on."

The following Tuesday was the Pennsylvania primary, and Swift called me at the statehouse to announce that Newton would report for duty the following Thursday.

"He'll be putting up at the Clark. I would appreciate it if you'd go over there Thursday night and give him dinner and bring him up to speed on our campaign coverage," Swift said.

"Dinner on expenses?"

"Of course, old boy," Swift said jovially. "We're going first cabin on this project."

Sure we were. I knew for a fact that the *Capital Register & Press* housed people at the Clark at half the going room rates. We also failed to mention the name of the hotel whenever one of the legislators who stayed there busted up the bar after a few too many or set fire to a mattress in his room. We might run a story, but the "where" in the story never was more precise than "a local hotel."

I called Newton from the Clark lobby at 6:00 P.M. Thursday.

"Come on up, chief," Newton boomed. "We're having a party."

He was in the governor's suite on the top floor, complete with two bedrooms, a kitchen and living room, and a balcony overlooking Capitol Circle. A lot of space for one person, but Newton had managed to kill the echo in a hurry. There were at least twenty people in the suite, including the state chairman of one political party, a former state House Speaker of the other, a gaggle of lobbyists, and a giggle of the flossy party girls who usually could be found at all major freeloads in town.

A fully stocked bar was getting heavy play and a finger food table already had been well worked over.

Naughton Newton, about forty, tall, skinny, and egg-bald,

was presiding over the festivities in the center of the living room. He was wearing high-top tennis shoes, once-white painter's bib overalls and no shirt. I knew from the stories that I had heard in past campaigns that this was one of his more conservative outfits. The jacket photo on his book showed him in a flak jacket and running shorts.

I slipped into the crowd around Newton and introduced myself.

"Glad to have you aboard, Bobby. Have a drink and a girl."

I got a drink, smiled at several girls, and settled back to watch. Newton was telling stories—probably within a mile or two of the truth—about the sexual preferences of the presidential candidates.

". . . and when he talks about his concern for the youth of the nation, it's a good idea to round up all the young boys in town and lock them in their rooms. But don't get me wrong, the senator will cheerfully corrupt a young girl if there's no boys available."

"Oh yes, the governor is well known for his opposition to capital punishment. But he's downright enthusiastic about corporal punishment. I understand he favors spanking, but has no objections to a little light whipping. Nothing to leave marks, though."

"Don't worry about the general. You won't catch him with his pants down. Fellow I know said he served on the old boy's staff in Korea, and the man was famous all over the peninsula as the fastest gun south of the Yalu—zipper down, gun on target, pow! The girls in Seoul called him the jet pilot."

Along about ten o'clock, the party seemed to be winding down. I decided to try to talk some business with Newton. He had been drinking ale and was still bright-eyed.

"Ah, Naughton," I said.

"Knocko, chief. I'd have changed it long ago, but I have

this rich uncle with the same name and if I dump Naughton, it's out of the old will I go. Knocko, please."

"Well, Knocko, I brought the tentative schedules we have for the candidates next week, and thought we might work out a travel schedule for you. Then we can assign the rest of our people around your plans."

"Oh God, Bobby, I don't work like that. I don't know what the hell I'm going to be doing half an hour from now let alone next week either. Just go ahead and assign your people and we'll play it by ear. You got any ladies covering the campaign?"

Cindy and Diana Osky, who usually did features, were going out on some candidate swings, but I used my head for once and ignored the question.

"Well, the M.E. suggested we assign one reporter to work directly with you . . . keeping track of the schedules and the travel and the copy filing and all. We've got Morrie Gealber lined up to work with you for the next two weeks. He's a business page reporter regularly, but a hell of an organizer. He asked me to see if you could give him a little lead time setting things up. That's why I thought we might do some planning tonight."

Newton looked like an American Legion conventioneer whose water pistol had just been confiscated.

"No girls, huh? Well, shit, you're the number one political guy, aren't you? I thought it was settled in advance you'd come with me. You know the locals and the candidates, don't you? I can't remember these guys' names after they get elected, let alone when they're just running for office."

Christ. Now I knew who was going to be the nurse.

I put my glass down and started to leave, but Knocko grabbed my arm.

"Hey, don't leave, chief. I've got the general's state coordinator coming up later and I need you to sit in. Want to make sure he doesn't try to bullshit me.

"Besides, we need to get some use out of this layout. I

checked out of the rat-trap single room your boss reserved for me and moved up here, so I'd have a proper place to do business. I mean, how would it look to ask the top aide of a presidential candidate to come up for an interview and have him sit on the bed? If you want a class product, you put on a class act, no?"

Me, I didn't argue. Swift was Newton's problem.

CHAPTER 11

Swift made no waves about Newton's $275-a-day suite. "He's used to such," Swift told me the next morning after I reported on his trained seal's first night in town. "Besides, we write it all off."

Sure. I wondered what kind of deal Swift had cut with the Clark manager on this one. Whatever it was, I was willing to bet a week's pay the paper wasn't paying full freight.

But Newton did make the most of his luxury digs, running a nonstop bar and summoning pols from both the state party and the candidates' campaign operations to interviews. He would sit down with each one, chat for five or ten minutes, and then leave them to fend for themselves. Women got more time; he spent forty-five minutes with the senator's state press coordinator—a good-looking brunette—and she was still there when I ended Saturday night on Sunday morning.

This went on all weekend and, to my observation, Newton never took a note and certainly never asked me for any information about the people he was talking to.

Sunday night, Newton shut down the bar and began shooing people out about 1:30 A.M. The crowd had grown as the word passed that free booze and a look at a celebrity were available at the Clark.

"Thirsty bunch you've got around here, Bobby. Hate to eighty-six anybody, but you look tired, and I want you in trim for tomorrow."

"Tomorrow?"

"Sure. Don't you remember that schedule you gave me? We're going campaigning tomorrow with the general. He's flying into the city at 8:00 A.M. and that means we've got to be on the road here by 6:30 to get to the airport on time. Pick me up in front of the hotel, OK?"

Inasmuch as Newton hadn't given me a clue that he intended to pay the least attention to the schedule I had offered, there were just a few small chores for me before I could sack out. I had to wake up Tandee and tell him we were traveling in the morning, at his angry demand go by the paper and get photo equipment and supplies, and book a rental car we could pick up in the morning and leave at the airport the next day when we joined the campaign. I also had to pack for myself, groping in the dresser to avoid turning on a light and waking Liz. I had it all in hand by 3:30 and got a full two hours' sleep.

No hitches the next morning. Tandee was ready, whining, of course, and Newton was pacing up and down in front of the hotel when we arrived at 6:25. He was wearing the same camouflage combat fatigues, sandals, and pinned-brim Anzac hat I had left him in five hours earlier and carrying a Bloomingdale's shopping bag packed to the brim. The clothes looked rumpled but Newton looked fresh as a dewy rose. He also looked hopping mad.

"You got a fuckin' Gestapo for cops in this town. Goddamn squad car pulled up when I came out of the hotel and told me they didn't allow bums to hang around the hotel. I had to get the desk clerk to vouch for me and keep the assholes from running me in."

Having delivered himself of that denunciation and nodded at the astonished Whine, Newton sprawled across the back seat and went to sleep. It took us about an hour to get to the airport and by the time we dumped the car, found the general's advance man at the private aircraft hangar, and got our bags tagged and credentials filled out, the candidate was on the ground.

We headed for the press bus, but Newton, spotting a wire service reporter he seemed to know, climbed into the pool car and gave us a cheery wave as we trudged toward the back of the motorcade lined up on the tarmac.

We did three stops that morning. The first was a grade school where the general told an auditorium full of kids that an active life of exercise and self-discipline was essential for them if they were to survive the coming nuclear holocaust. He led them in ten minutes of aerobics. One of the teachers had to be given CPR, but the general wasn't breathing hard, and the kids were delighted.

Next was a senior citizens' center where he announced his administration would form a home guard for men aged sixty and older: "Slackers will lose their social security," he said with a wolfish smile. He tried to organize more aerobics, but the medical director of the place threatened to call the cops and charge the general with malicious endangerment.

The last stop before we were given thirty minutes to find lunch and to file copy was the Flugbach Brewery, where the general chug-a-lugged a quart like it was lemonade, gave an immense belch to the delight of the workers on the bottling line, and declared he was getting tired of seeing all the Kraut beer being sold in the United States while our people were being laid off.

"If we can require Jap cars sold in this country to have American parts, we can oblige the Huns to use American grain in their beer and bottle it over here," he bellowed. He was cheered wildly.

Our break was in a recreation room at the brewery, which set up a line of kegs and poured for all comers, including the traveling press corps. It looked like lunch was going to be liquid barley, malt, and hops. Newton had been given (or had swiped) a huge ornate ceramic mug with a tip-up pewter lid, and he spent the half hour with his nose immersed in it.

I called the paper with some quick dictation, and before I had finished, Swift came on the line.

"This doesn't look like Naughton Newton's stuff, Wartovsky. Where is his copy?"

I glanced helplessly at Newton, who was getting a third refill, and told Swift, "He's writing. You can't expect him to dictate his kind of material off the cuff. We'll call from the next stop."

Newton's burp when I told him about Swift's demand matched the general's. "Jesus, he's some kind of fever blister, ain't he? Didn't you say we've got until 6 P.M. to file? Next chance you get, call and tell him I'll have two columns before the deadline. Three, if he wants it."

That was going to be a trick, because our next stop was 350 miles north of the city at the far end of the state. We got back into the motorcade, drove to the airport, and piled into the Boeing 727 charter the general was using.

Painted on the nose of the plane was "Jacta alea est." My Latin being what it wasn't, when we got settled in our seats I asked the guy across the aisle if he knew what it meant.

"The *New York Times* man said it's what Caesar said when he crossed the Rubicon—'The die is cast.' The guy from the *Daily News* said that may be what the quote says, but that ain't what Caesar said. He claims old Julius got to the river and found his quartermaster had forgotten to bring boats and said, 'The shit is going to hit the fan.'"

Newton was sitting next to me with his seat reclined to its limit and his hat tipped over his face. The stewardess came by and asked him to raise the seat during the takeoff, which was imminent. Newton emitted a long snore. She reached over and raised his hat and jumped a foot to the accompaniment of a high-C yelp. Somewhere during the morning Newton had picked up a rubber mask of Jabba the Hut. She decided to leave him alone.

After we got off the ground, the general came back into the press section and allowed that he had done well in the morning and expected great things of this swing through the state.

Someone asked him if it was true that when he was in the Pentagon he had developed a plan to base MX missiles on the Strip in Las Vegas.

"Best plan I ever had," the general replied. "Everywhere else the namby-pamby civilians were crying about how the birds were going to destroy their patio cookouts and give fish and wild geese anxiety attacks or something.

"So I picked the one place in the country where a major missile launch wouldn't disturb anyone. Hell, we used to do atomic tests just down the road from Vegas and it never bothered the players. But those lily-livered politicians in the secretary's office vetoed it—claimed it was an unwarranted intrusion on the private sector. I think Howard Hughes threatened to refuse to pay his taxes if we went ahead with it."

The general turned to go back to the front of the plane, but stopped and said, "You camera boys. I'm going to take over the controls for a while. Come along if you want some pictures."

The photogs stampeded into the front of the plane. They took turns in the cockpit and after ten minutes Whine came back.

"Did you get it?" Newton asked as Whine slipped by to his seat.

"Right here," Whine said, patting the camera.

"Give me the roll," Newton said in a low voice.

"What'dya mean?"

"Give me the film, damn it."

Whine rolled up the film, opened the camera, and handed Newton the cartridge. He put it under his hat, which he tipped back over his face.

A few minutes later, half a dozen other photographers came back, followed by the traveling press secretary and the pilot. From the gabbling, it seemed that something was wrong.

"Listen up, everybody." the press guy said. "We made a goof with this thing about the general flying the plane. He's qualified on jets, but he doesn't have a passenger certificate, and it's going to be six kinds of hell if it gets in the papers. So please, will the writers forget about it and the camera guys just throw away the film."

Nobody said anything. The pilot stepped in front of the press secretary. "This is important, guys. If this gets out, I'll probably get grounded and technically the general could be charged with a federal crime. If you won't do it for me and the general, think how long you might be stuck up in the north woods until the airline gets a substitute pilot up here. Could be days."

Groans and curses filled the cabin, but first one and then half a dozen photographers pulled the film out of their cameras and passed it to the press secretary. Whine nudged Newton, who tipped up his hat, reached down in Whine's bag, and handed an unexposed film cartridge into the aisle. He grinned and went back into his felt shell.

"And the writers . . . will all you guys keep this dark?"

There was a mumble of "OKs," and the pilot and the secretary returned to the forward compartment.

It was about 3:30 when we landed, and Newton touched my arm as we were leaving the plane.

"I'm not going on the motorcade. I'll see you when you get back."

Newton slipped out of the line for the bus and disappeared into the terminal. As I went up the steps of the bus, I could see him leaning over the air express desk.

We were in transit about seven hours, making about four stops for speeches and ending up with a long and boring banquet and not much news. It was dark when we got back to the airport, but a couple hundred of the general's supporters were waiting for a final word from the great man. He got up on a platform, did about five minutes of thank you's, and then paused, groping for a final word.

"We enjoyed our time here, and it was made more pleasant by the fact that we were flown here by a native of this area. Captain Crockhorn, come on up here."

The pilot started to climb the steps and the general went on: "The captain is a fine and generous man as well as a skillful aviator. Why, he even let an old fighter jockey like me handle his plane on our way here."

The pilot stopped with one foot suspended—a look of horror on his face. One of the photographers blurted out, "Oh, shit!" and a couple of reporters started back for the terminal, but it was too late. The general climbed down from the platform and went up the steps of the plane. The press secretary, yelled, "Takeoff in four minutes," and everybody ran for the plane.

Newton already was aboard, regaling the stewardess he had earlier caused to nearly wet her pants with some cock-and-bull story—about being the last American to leave Iran—and his trek across the desert to escape the clutches of the Ayatollah.

He grinned at Whine and me as we sat down. Over the racket of photographers and reporters yelling unprintables at the press secretary, he muttered, "The film got to the paper. They're going to use it on the front page with my story about the general violating the civil aviation laws."

I knew the wraps were off the story now, but they sure weren't when Newton wrote it.

"But we promised not to write it," I said.

"Not me," Newton said, leaning back in his seat. "I was asleep."

We got back to the city just after 11:00—too late for most of the others in the plane to get much either in their papers or on the air. It was a good story, but not really big enough to warrant tearing up front pages or news shows.

But, of course, Swift played the story like the Second Coming, which panicked the late night people at the wire service bureaus when they saw the first edition in the capital. They banged out bell-ringing stories, which in turn woke up the night side telegraph editors all the way to the East Coast and, from what I heard later, resulted in a half dozen or so 2:00 A.M. telephone calls demanding matching stories from the reporters who had been with the campaign. Most of them were too groggy to do more than mumble, "Pick up the wires." Some did and the *Capital Register & Press* got mentioned high up because Swift had copyrighted the story just in case anyone thought to run the story without credit.

We didn't have to explain to anyone the next morning. We were enroute at 7:00 A.M. for Barnwell, where we were picking up the senator's campaign. Swift had left a note at the hotel desk, congratulating Newton.

Newton read the note to us as we rolled out of town.

"I wonder what it's going to be like on the general's press bus this morning," Whine said.

Newton's face creased in an evil grin. "The *Daily News* was right about that slogan," he said.

We also got lucky when we hooked up with the senator. His traveling press secretary turned out to be an old drinking buddy of Newton's, and he booked Knocko for a one-on-one interview with the candidate that afternoon. This was something of a coup because the senator had been dodging interviews for more than a week. He had given a girl from one of the New York tabs an hour, and she wrote a piece that gave the distinct impression that he had put a move on her in his compartment in the plane.

"Couldn't have been," the press secretary told us. "He's been nursing a bad back for weeks. By the time we get back to the plane after a day of rutabaga festivals and prize goat shows, he's so beat he can't get up on his feet, let alone anything else.

"And hey, Knocko. Don't go getting me in trouble. I told him you would be asking him about the campaign. He strictly ain't talking about his divorce, and he definitely ain't talking about the ladies he's been seeing since."

"I'll be the soul of discretion," Newton replied. "You know you can trust me, buddy."

That morning, the senator toured a lawn mower factory, trying to grin as he climbed up on the seat of the deluxe rider with automatic bagger, turbo-jet mulcher, and built-in six-pack cooler.

We got a few minutes to file at the airport after a couple more stops and then took off again for the other end of the state. When we got off the ground, the press guy came back, crooked his finger at Newton and led him and Whine up to the front of the plane toward the candidate's sanctum.

When they left, Dick Clayton came over and sat next to me.

Clayton was one of the best known political reporters in the country—a dozen times a year on "Meet the Press" and the other Sunday gab shows—but he never acted like he was somebody special. I had watched him in other campaigns and, unlike some in the traveling national press rat pack, he made a point of spending time with the local reporters.

Clayton did it because he really was a nice guy, but he also got a dividend out of those chats. He had built a network of friends and admirers all over the country he could call from Washington when he needed a quick fill on some state or local political situation. Reporters who were reluctant to share information with their own editors fell all over themselves to accommodate Clayton. Hell, I once gave him the vacation phone number of our speaker, and I'm pretty sure I was the only person who had it besides his bookie. At least, that's what the bookie said.

"Knocko got an interview with Himself." It was a comment, not a question. I started to reply, but Clayton raised his hand. "No big deal. I know he's been buddies with Jackie Corley from way back. Besides, not much is happening on this campaign to ask about. I'm switching to the general day after tomorrow."

This time, Clayton waited for a response.

"We just left that campaign," I said.

"So I heard from the press people over there when I phoned to make arrangements to join them. I didn't get the picture of a very happy press corps this morning." Clayton paused and gave me a long look.

"Bob, let me tell you something. I think, and so do a lot of others, that Knocko is beginning to lose his amusement value. Back in the seventies, he was fun to watch because he did and said and wrote wild stuff that the rest of us wished we could get away with or had the guts to try. But he's trying to outdo himself every four years and it's getting beyond funny. It's getting sick and I think maybe dangerous.

"From what I hear, you're pretty much stuck with him, and I know damn well nobody can keep him on the ground once he gets going. But don't let Knocko leave you with a lap full of broken eggs. He's going to leave after the primary, but you've got to work in this state. Just some advice—don't play patsy for him."

Clayton gave me a pat on the shoulder and went back to his seat. Just before the plane started its landing approach, Knocko and Whine returned. As they settled into their seats, Newton took something out of his pocket and shoved it into the shopping bag he carried wherever he went.

We did a couple of stops and the senator really looked like he was in pain. He had a thirty-minute break in midafternoon and went through another three appearances without apparent discomfort, although he seemed somewhat distracted. Newton, who usually didn't follow along close to the candidate in the mob scenes before, during, and after these campaign events, was right up with the TV crews and wire service people all day.

We were ending the day back in the city and planned to file from there. When we got back to the hotel and checked in, Newton called me from his room.

"Give old Ironpants Swift a call and tell him I'll be filing in half an hour, will you, chief? Also, come on down when you can. I've got a ball-buster story and I may need you to dictate while I write."

I was getting a little bit more than tired of being a copy boy, but Swift wasn't likely to be sympathetic if I bitched. So I went down to Newton's room and found him flailing away at the portable typewriter I'd brought on the trip. He handed me the first two pages and turned back to the keyboard.

The hair went up on the back of my neck when I read the lead:

By NAUGHTON NEWTON
Exclusive to *The Capital Register & Press*

Sen. Vernon Raglinton, a front-running candidate for the presidential nomination of his party and a pillar of the Washington establishment, is under treatment for a mental disorder, *The Capital Register & Press* learned Tuesday.

"Are you nuts?" I shouted at Newton.

"Not me, him. Read on, Bobby," Newton said as he continued to type.

The senator, campaigning in the state for the primary next week, is being treated by doctors with a derivative of phenothiazine, a drug used to control psychoses, this newspaper learned.

The drug, sold under various trade names, is regarded as "a highly potent behavior modifier" and is widely used in mental institutions to treat patients whose extreme mood swings make conventional psychotherapy difficult.

The senator's erratic behavior was observed first-hand by this reporter during a number of campaign appearances in the northern part of the state. He was seen to exhibit various symptoms of discomfort, nervousness, and inappropriate gaiety at early stops in his campaign swing, but later in the day appeared relaxed and somewhat disoriented.

This reporter was able during the course of the day to establish that the senator had a supply of the antipsychotic drug on his chartered jet airplane. It was believed he used the medication during a rest stop, after his first appearances of the day and after which his behavior changed markedly.

"This is crazy shit," I yelled. "You don't know he's on that drug!"

Newton turned from the typewriter. "The hell I don't," he said. He dug into the bulging shopping bag and came up with an amber plastic vial. He tossed it to me.

"Mellaril," he said. "Used in the best laughing academies. That's an empty I found in the trash bin in the head next to Raglinton's compartment. You can be damn sure he has more in his luggage.

"Now let's get going with the story. Call the paper and start dictating."

"Not me," I said. "You can't call a presidential candidate crazy on what you have. I'm not going to have anything to do with this." I all but ran out of the room.

I went down to the bar and had a beer. This was the worst yet. I could just imagine what Swift was going to do with this story. I thought of calling him and trying to talk him out of using it without some better documentation, but decided he'd just blow his top at me. But Clayton was right; I wasn't going to be the patsy.

After a second beer, I took my bill and as I dug in my pocket for money, found I still had the plastic vial. Out in the better light of the hotel lobby, I read the label.

It was from a Washington pharmacy and had the senator's name typed in. At the bottom, it had the dosage and the drug name. One look and I sprinted to the elevator.

I pounded on Newton's door for what seemed like five minutes before he finally opened it. He had a drink in his hand and a silly smile on his face. The windows of the room were open and a strong breeze was blowing the curtains. Even so, you could smell the pot.

"Story's in," he mumbled. "Didn't need you."

"What drug did you say came in this?" I demanded, shoving the vial at him.

Newton looked at me vacantly. "I forget. Oh yeah, Mellaril. Powerful shit, man."

"Look at the bottle. That says Flexaril."

Newton studied the pill container. "Oh shit, they got dozens of names for this stuff. Same thing from a different company. I ought to know. . . ." He stopped in midsentence and then smiled.

"Now come on, let's celebrate. I ain't mad at you. You just got spooked by a big story. Like I always tell these tight-ass turkeys that cover these campaigns and all the time bitch about having to cover the same speech every day, you can always find a good story if you just show some enterprise."

I walked out this time. I went to my room and packed and decided that when the campaign got to the capital tomorrow, I was leaving it and Newton, even if it cost me my job. Swift could baby-sit this maniac.

The bus was scheduled to leave for the airport at 8:30 the next morning, but when I got to the lobby, Jackie Corley was stopping reporters and directing them to a meeting room.

"Press conference before we leave, Wartovsky. Where's that asshole you're traveling with?"

"I don't know," I replied. "He'll be down."

The senator was standing at the front of the room with another man. Both of them looked tired and grim.

When the room was nearly full, Corley came to the door and said, "We can start now, senator." As I looked back, I saw Newton leaning against the wall, smiling.

"I'm going to make this short because I know some of you have early afternoon paper deadlines, and we have a schedule to make," the senator said.

"Some of you know a newspaper in this state published a story this morning that made certain allegations about my health—my mental health. They were totally and viciously false. I have instructed my attorneys to take legal action against the writer and the newspaper.

"But I also know my denial and my decision to take legal action may appear self-serving to some. After learning of this story late last night and in the hope of nipping this malicious business in the bud, I asked my personal physician, Dr. Gordon Flaring, to fly from Washington. He arrived just half an hour ago. Doctor?"

The white-haired man with the senator stepped forward. "I have been the senator's physician for eighteen years. I can say with complete assurance that he does not and never has suffered from any psychosis, neurosis, or disease that could be called a mental disorder."

The doctor reached into a small, flat briefcase. "With the senator's permission, I have brought his medical records. They cover the entire period I have treated him, and they include reports from all other doctors who have examined or treated him. I have attached an affidavit affirming that this is the complete medical history of Senator Raglinton and stating what I just told you about his health.

"I am told the hotel has duplicating facilities that will allow each of you to have a copy of this material within fifteen minutes.

"But before I send these to be copied, I wish to make one thing clear. I have been treating the senator in the last two weeks for a condition that could be called in lay language, pulled muscles of the lower back. I prescribed for that condition a drug called Flexaril to relieve the distress. It also sometimes causes drowsiness, and patients who take it are advised not to drive automobiles or operate machinery. For the record, its chemical name is cyclobenzaprine hydrochloride. It is not an antipsychotic drug. It is a muscle relaxant."

I looked at Newton. He was still smiling, for God's sake.

The press conference ended and I called the paper from a pay phone in the lobby. Swift wasn't in his office, and I gave Grace the nub of what the senator and the doctor had said. Corley came by with a sheaf of the medical report copies and said the bus was leaving for the airport, but we would have time there to file before taking off for the capital.

I climbed into the bus and took a seat on the window near the front. I was starting to leaf through the medical report when I saw Newton emerging from the hotel with a brimming paper cup of coffee in one hand and the portable typewriter and the ever-present shopping bag in the other.

Dick Clayton and several other reporters were behind Newton. As Newton began to step into the bus, Clayton said, "Here, Knocko, let me help you." He took the typewriter and the bag from Newton, who turned abruptly, sloshing hot coffee on his hand.

Clayton put the typewriter on the ground and upended the shopping bag. Out came a wad of wrinkled clothes, a half-empty bottle of bourbon, assorted toilet articles, and a pint mason jar, which shattered as it hit the pavement. A small pile of brownish material poured out. Mixed in were half a dozen fat hand-rolled cigarettes.

Clayton reached down and picked up one of the cigarettes, holding it under his nose.

"Smells like good Colombian, Knocko. I knew we would be able to get a better story out of this than some routine press conference." He smiled broadly at Newton. "If we only showed some enterprise, of course."

CHAPTER 12

Newton jammed his belongings, sans the pile of pot, into the Bloomies bag and climbed aboard the bus. He sat down next to me and for once, he wasn't grinning.

"Jealous bastards," he said, staring straight ahead.

Before I could say anything, Clayton came back to our row and hunkered down in the aisle next to Newton.

"Knocko, I don't know what the rest of these guys are going to do, but I'm filing a story about Raglinton denying there is anything funny about his head contrary to published reports. I'm not going to go into how or who published them. The medical report has enough in it to fill out a piece, and I guess now we'll be getting them from the other candidates—the general's bunions and the governor's football knee, I suppose."

Newton looked at him. "See, Dick, I did everybody a service."

"Bullshit, Knocko. I'm telling you I'm not going to nail you this time and some of the others may go along for old times' sake. But that's it, mister. You pull that kind of stunt one more time on this campaign, and I'm going to do a boys on the bus piece with you as the stoned star. I don't know if you'll get any more campaign jobs, but I can damn well guarantee you you'll have narcs shaking you down every time you step off a plane."

"Don't fucking threaten me," Newton snarled.

"No threat," Clayton said, standing up. "It's a legitimate

story, and you know damn well it'll get the whole pack baying on the same trail."

Clayton walked back to his seat, and Newton said nothing more until the bus reached the airport. As we pulled alongside the senator's charter, Newton turned to me, the smile back on his face.

"Well, chief, this is it. I'm dropping off here."

"Leaving?" I said. "I thought you were going to stay through the primary."

"Change of plans. Tell old Swift I got an urgent call from my Aunt Matilda that my Uncle Naughton has taken deathly ill. Got to rush to the old boy's bedside. Family ties and all."

As I got to the top of the stairs going into the plane, I saw Newton, lugging his bag, heading toward the taxi stand in the charter terminal. I spent the short flight back to the capital, where the senator had a rally at the state college, rehearsing what I would say to Swift.

The senator had a crowd waiting for him at the airport and Liz was there to take pictures. I skipped the bus and walked with her to the company car, where she gave me a long kiss.

"Boy, have I missed you."

"Good. I think after what's happened, I'll be home for a while."

"That's good, too. I was going to call you—something funny has been going on."

"At the paper?"

"As usual. But I mean at your apartment building. I was coming home the other night and saw that lunk friend of Kirk Bright's coming out of the building. I thought I saw him driving away yesterday morning, too. I don't think he saw me either time."

"Kehler? What the hell could he have been doing at my place? I think he and Kirk live in that new condo building by the river."

"I don't know, Bob, but he scares me. He looks as though he couldn't light up a fifteen-watt bulb, but he's got the meanest way of looking at you I've ever seen—like he's just waiting for an excuse to use those ham hands on you. Anyway, I was going to stay at my place tonight if you were going to go out with the campaign."

I didn't much relish the idea of running into Kenny Kehler in an unfriendly situation either, but I took the macho stance with Liz.

"Has he said anything to you? At the Next Door? Maybe he's one of these crazies that likes to track girls."

"No. He hasn't said word one to me, even when we were sitting at the same table. I don't think he pays attention to anyone except Kirk. Like a dog sitting at its master's feet or something. But I don't think Kirk's gay . . . he's dating at least two women at the paper."

"Well, whatever Kehler's up to, he'll probably steer clear now that I'm back. If not, we'll have the cops on him."

We arrived at the paper and I went in while Liz parked the car.

I glanced at that day's paper in the vending box outside the building. Swift had chosen a picture of the senator taken during one of his more energetic speeches. It showed him flailing his arms, his hair flying, and his mouth wide open. It was correctly calculated to make him look nuts and, as always, the headlines were even more fevered than the story if that was possible.

SENATOR USING
PSYCHO PILLS

CANDIDATE TAKING
MENTAL MEDICINE

Swift wasn't in his office, so I went to an empty desk and started a story on the senator's press conference and his rally when he arrived in the capital. I led with the rally, telling myself it was the freshest stuff and the local angle, even if it wasn't the newsiest event of the day. In truth, I figured Swift wasn't about to print a piece with a lead knocking down our own front page exposé.

I was wrong again. Swift came up behind me as I was working on the piece and said, "Put the stuff about the senator denying he's taking that drug at the top. Do a full piece on the press conference. Direct quotes if you taped it."

I turned to look at him.

"We're backing off Knocko's piece?"

"Have to. I've just spent an hour in Shiu's office with the lawyers. From what the wires carried this morning, that bloody Newton bollixed the piece completely. Fetched us a whopping libel threat. We're running a separate retraction too, and the lawyers think the senator will just let it drop there. The bugger must have been drunk again."

He stepped back and looked around the newsroom. "And where the hell is he?"

I told Swift about the episode at the bus that morning and Newton's sudden decision to clear out. Another surprise; he didn't seem all that upset.

"Just as well. The lawyers told me to send him packing or at least keep his stuff out of the paper for the rest of the time we've got him on contract. Now we'll just pay him off through yesterday and be well rid of him."

Without thinking about it, I took a chance with Swift. "I thought you admired his work."

Swift sat down on the edge of the desk. "I did and I do. He is one of the few American reporters I've seen who is willing to go for the big play, and when he finds it, knows how to write it. Of course, that means taking chances and sometimes mucking up a story. That's the price you pay and this time we're paying it.

"The reason I sent you along with him was to give us some insurance against Newton's well-known affection for the bottle—and the weed, from what you tell me now—and keep him somewhere near the ground. He told me yesterday you walked out on him, but he seemed so sure about the story that I let it go. You didn't call to argue about it. By the way, why not?"

This is what I had been thinking about on the plane, and I had come to the conclusion that it was time to stop imitating a bowl of Jell-O every time I dealt with Swift.

"This may be my job, Mr. Swift, but I figured you were going to run whatever Newton wrote, and nothing I could say would tout you off him. The guy is a total flake. I don't think he has the foggiest idea what is going on in politics nor gives a damn . . . and I'm not sure you do either."

It was out and I expected so would I be in the next minute. But Swift had a mild expression behind all the whiskery growth.

"Bob, cool down. I can understand why you feel that way and to some extent it is true that I don't know or care about what you and your confreres call the nuts and bolts of politics.

"I knew my man when I hired Newton. I didn't want another dead serious, political science analysis of the primary campaign. I wanted something with excitement and zing in it—and you have to admit I got it. I knew it was a risk to take Newton on and it was my responsibility, not yours, to keep him from going too far. You probably are right that I would have run the piece even if you had registered an objection. He seemed to have the story cold, and I would have been hard put to dump it. As your President Truman had it, the buck stops here."

I told Swift about my discovery that Newton had read or copied the name of the senator's drug wrong and about Knocko's refusal to accept the possibility that he had made a mistake.

Swift sighed and looked over the newsroom.

"I think perhaps I am looking for something here that I won't find. I've been in this business for thirty-odd years and only once or twice have I found people who have the knack I seek. Some reporters and writers and editors have what I would call a natural bent for the situations and the language facility that make people who buy newspapers sit up and pay attention. Just as born salesmen seem to know instinctively how to approach and persuade, I am looking for newspeople who know without fail the 'buttons' that command readership and when to push them.

"I like to think I have that knack myself and a feeling for others that do as well. The first week I sat down at a copy desk the paper had a story about a controversy over a picture the local museum had acquired—a very explicit figure painting. Some local politician had pronounced it pornographic, and our reporter went to the mayor for comment which he declined. The moment I looked at the story I saw the headline: 'Mayor Mute on New Nude.' Egotistically, I thought that was a classic headline. But when I began seeing the work of real professionals, I realized it was at best a fair first effort. The best I've seen was in the *New York Post* a few years back—'Headless Body Found in Topless Bar.' Someday I will better that."

I had swiveled in my chair to face Swift and he paused, looking embarrassed, like a man surprised while talking to himself. He smiled faintly and continued.

"That's the kind of quality I was looking for in Newton. It's more of an instinct or a reflex than any learned response— the quick and sure knowledge that certain kinds of people and behavior and events described in certain words will lift everyday situations out of the mundane and make them exciting. Exciting, damn it!"

Swift's eyes were almost glowing, and he clapped his hands sharply to emphasize his last point.

"You're talking about yellow journalism," I said.

"Indeed, and disabuse yourself of any notion that the epithet bothers me in the least," Swift said. "It made mass-circulation newspapers possible and, I like to think, it made people who wouldn't otherwise pay attention to anything other than their own immediate personal concerns and needs at least partially aware of what was going on beyond the sight of their own limited horizons.

"Let me tell you, I am not one who believes the twaddle that man is inherently a noble creature. I believe people, most people, are driven by two rather simple motivations that go back to the cave. Fear. That's why so many work at jobs they abhor to feed and clothe and shelter themselves. Lust. Nature's way to impel us to reproduce. Greed and jealousy—functions of fear and lust. The higher intellectual and emotional motivations, as we might call them, are taught—and in crisis, when survival is at stake, sloughed off.

"Look at your own American story of the Donner party, reduced to cannibalism when the choice was to survive or conform to so-called civilized values. And the same thing happened just a few years ago when that plane crashed in South America.

"My point in this, old boy, is that we can prattle on all we want about the holy mission of journalism and about the people's right to know, but at bottom we succeed only when we serve the perceived needs of those who plunk down a quarter for what we produce. Yes, there are many who want to know about the plight of the snail darter and the artistic triumphs of the New York Philharmonic, and there are newspapers and magazines and television networks to give them what they want. But there are many, many more who want to read about crimes of passion and the foibles of the high and mighty—about dotty senators, if you will. I did not make it that way, but I recognize it as reality, and it doesn't make me feel guilty or debased to serve those people. And I don't give a moldy fig for the elitists in our business who think I should."

This, I figured, didn't really require a response, unless it was going to be good-bye. "Well, I guess my reality is that I better get cracking on this piece. Grace looks like he's getting antsy."

"Yes. I have some things that need attention as well."

I rewrote the story about the senator, checked with Grace to make sure we both had the same marching orders, and went off to the Next Door to see if Liz was around.

She was, sitting at a table where Farley Free was holding forth to a half dozen or so of the staff.

". . . so I told him, this story isn't going to win us any popularity contests. But he's a stubborn son of a bitch. The piece is going to be at the top of the sports page tomorrow."

"What now?" I asked, sliding a chair up to the table.

"Oh shit, Bob, I walked into one with that bastard Swift. We got word today that the fullback at Central High had been dropped from the team without explanation. They're having their spring practice to get things lined up for next season. I did some checking and found out that the kid had made a pass at the tight end in the shower.

"I talked to the coach and the principal and both said it was the first time, but the kid admitted he'd had homosexual impulses for a long time and agreed that he couldn't very well stay on the team after this incident. Both the coach and the principal said that was going to be the end of it, so I decided, what the hell, who was it going to help to label the kid a queer, not to mention we had nothing official to back it up.

"So, thinking the good sports editor keeps his M.E. up to date, I told Swift I was going to run a piece about the kid being fired from the team and say it was for breaking training rules. Like I should have expected, he hit the roof and insisted we do a story with the homosexual angle—a big story—and the head he wrote for it, God! 'Gay Back Gets Sack.'"

We chewed that over a while and I gave a play-by-play of my adventures with Knocko. By the time we got up and left, it was near nine, and I was running on empty.

Liz drove us home and as we opened the door, the phone was ringing. I picked it up and it was the most excited Frank Sanders I had heard to date.

"Bob! Where the hell have you been? Listen, we've got the break we've been waiting for. My source down in Chicago came through. I've got the proof—on paper—that the mob owns the CR&P—and the plans for what they are going to do with it."

"Go broke paying libel settlements, probably," I offered.

"Oh, you mean the story about the senator. Hell, he's not about to sue and get the story one paper ran into the court records, so any paper can safely run it. Besides, with Knocko's name on it, the CR&P can plead innocent by reason of insanity.

"But listen up, Bob, I need some stuff from you and Liz before I can get started on this. Can you get me copies of the incorporation papers? And anything on that helicopter—you know, any licenses or documents on file, maybe at the airport?"

"Sure, I'll get what I can together tomorrow."

"And tell Liz I need photos of Shiu and Swift if there are any in the files. She shouldn't try to take new ones—too much chance of spooking them. Also, if she took anything of the helicopter . . . it turns out to be an important part of all this."

"Yeah? How?" I asked.

"I'll fill you both in tomorrow night if you'll bring the stuff up here. If you can leave after five, you can be up here in time for dinner—a victory dinner. I'm buying."

Liz had been head-to-head with me listening. She nodded and I told Frank we'd see him about 7:30. Liz walked over to the window of the apartment as I hung up and started for the bedroom.

"Bob! Come here! There's that Kenny again!"

I went to the window to see a car pulling out of a parking place on the side street two stories below. The angle was too acute to have any chance of reading a license plate number.

"You're sure it was Kehler? It's pretty dark down there."

"He was in the bar tonight before you came in. He was

wearing a black-and-white-checked jacket. That's what I saw out the window."

She paused, a frightened look on her face. "Bob, he came out of the side entrance of this building—the basement entrance."

All thought of sleep vanished. Carrying a flashlight and a softball bat that had been deposited in the back of a closet years ago, we went down to the building cellar. There was no sign that anyone was or had been there. I found the telephone junction box in a corner. It had no lock and opened easily, but there was nothing in it that looked wrong and nothing that indicated it had been tampered with.

"Look." Liz pointed at several gray clumps on the floor. We bent down. I shined the flashlight on them. They were cigarette ashes—their cylindrical form still intact. Liz blew at one and it scattered into powder. "Unless this place is airtight, those things are fresh," she said.

Not sure proof, but enough for me. "Come on, we've got to call Frank back."

Frank's phone didn't answer. We tried again at ten o'clock and at eleven. We debated setting out for the university town right then, but decided there was no sense going off half-cocked. Liz told me to get some sleep and she would keep trying to call. I was only dimly aware when she crawled into bed and said in my ear, "I got him. He said not to worry."

The next morning over coffee, Liz said she finally got through to Frank just after midnight. "He sounded a little uptight, but kept saying he was all right. He just said 'Uh huh' when I told him about Kehler and what we found in the basement. Oh, he also said I should remind you to look up Mr. Murphy today."

"Murphy? What Murphy? He didn't tell me anything about a Murphy."

"Bob, I don't know. That's just what he said."

Liz had the day off, but wanted to use the car so she drove me to work. We were in front of the paper when I remembered. I didn't have to look up Murphy.

I told Liz to wait where she was and went to a pay phone in the lobby of the paper. I put in a collect call to Frank. The phone rang eight times before the operator came back on. "Your number does not answer, sir. Shall I place the call later?"

I called the city desk and left word for Grace that I was taking the day off as comp time for the overtime I put in on the campaign. I ran back outside where Liz was double-parked, shooed her over to the passenger side and headed the car for the interstate north. Liz waited for me to tell her what we were doing.

"Murphy. He was talking about Reg Murphy, the Atlanta editor who was kidnapped a few years back. Liz, I think they got him."

It was 10:30 when we got to Frank's building just a block from the campus. The apartment door was locked; there was no answer to the door chime. Liz knew the student janitor of the building and routed him, grumbling out of his basement apartment, to let us into Frank's place. He went back to his spherical trigonometry, and we were left in the empty apartment.

"Why don't you call the school to make sure he's not there," I said. While she was phoning, I looked through the apartment. There was nothing that looked as if there had been trouble. The bed was made, there were washed dishes on the kitchen drainboard, and the desk in the living room was in comparatively good order. There was nothing on it or in the drawers that appeared to be about the CR&P. One of the desk drawers, fitted for file folders, was empty.

Liz put down the phone. "His office line doesn't answer and the department secretary says she hasn't heard from him. But she says he doesn't have any classes until later in the day, and he often doesn't come in until late."

"God, I don't know, Liz. I looked around and didn't see anything suspicious. I looked through the desk and couldn't find anything except that empty file drawer."

"That drawer is where he keeps files on his current work and the desk is always locked when he isn't working," Liz said. "Even when he's here he locks it when he finishes. Bob, we better call the police."

She picked up the phone again. I put my hand on her arm.

"Wait a minute, Liz. He told us this was a kidnapping. Maybe we ought to wait to hear from whoever took him."

"No way. I'm calling the cops."

I had an idea. "OK, I guess you're right. But if we have to explain why he may have been kidnapped, his investigation will be blown. How about this? You remember I told you about Bill Phlager, the county D.A. who helped with the Schmid story? He's down at the capital now, an assistant attorney general. How about I call him first and lay this out, so we can maybe get some help on how we should do this."

Liz nodded. She was scared and doing well to keep back the tears.

I called the attorney general's office and asked for Phlager. Arlene, who presided over the telephones, apparently didn't recognize my voice or was feeling unusually officious that morning.

"Who may I say is calling, please," she intoned.

"Bob Wartovsky. It's urgent."

"May I tell him what the call concerns, please?" She was playing games with me. Maybe it had something to do with the after-work drink I had been offering her but never got around to making definite.

"For Christ's sake, Arlene, it's important!"

"Sir, there is no call for obscene language."

"Arlene, tell Bill Phlager his blackmailer is calling him and he's behind in his payments."

Liz stared at me as if I had lost my mind as a great gust of laughter came back over the phone.

"Oh, Bob," Arlene choked out. "You crumb, you've made my day. I'll put you through."

I talked to Phlager for about twenty-five minutes. He interrupted only to ask several short questions and was ready at the end of the story with a short list of instructions.

"First, don't touch another thing in that apartment. I'm going to call the chief of police there, and I want both of you to sit down and wait until he or a ranking officer arrives. If they send the campus cops, ask them to call me immediately.

"Second, don't tell anyone what you've just told me until I get there. I'm going in to see the A.G. when I hang up, and I should be on the way in half an hour in a state police car.

"Third, if anyone calls with demands about Sanders, listen to them, take notes—see if he has a recorder around—but try to stall off any arrangements for ransom or whatever.

"And fourth, I hope I really don't have to tell you this—don't call your paper or talk to any press about this. Nobody, understand?"

"How about the foundation he was working for?"

"You think they can get him back? Nobody, Bob."

Within fifteen minutes, the deputy chief of the university town police was sitting with us. One officer was photographing the apartment; another was dusting fingerprint powder.

"Did you move anything?" the deputy chief asked. "Try to remember just what you did and where you were before you called Mr. Phlager."

Phlager got there within two hours. Larry Creston, who headed criminal investigation for the state police, was with him. We had done business before.

Creston went to one side with the deputy chief and Phlager sat down with us.

"We've got bulletins out in four states to look out for Sanders and Kehler. The car description . . . can you remember any more about the car?"

We weren't even sure about the color. We knew it was a big—probably American—sedan.

"The attorney general is calling the Chicago police and the FBI himself. Larry Creston is in charge of the police work; I'm the liaison. I've got to tell you, it will be a miracle if we find them on the road. If Kehler was here at midnight and they got out of here after Miss Sanders called, they almost surely are holed up by now.

"Another thing. Kehler is a mean customer. We know he worked five years as muscle for Gene Bright, but he hasn't been active for the last two years. We're not sure who he's with now. He's got a long sheet—as a kid he did a couple of terms for armed robbery and assault. He's a fist and foot boy basically, but he will use a gun and we rate him dangerous.

"Creston and I talked about this on the way up; about all we can do is keep looking for them without going public and wait for something from Kehler or whoever he's acting for."

Liz interrupted. "If we keep it secret, somebody might see them and not know Daddy has been kidnapped."

Creston had joined us. "It's a tradeoff, Miss. There is a chance someone may come forward with a lead, but there is also the chance that Kehler will panic and . . . uh, dispose of Professor Sanders. For now, we best be quiet about it."

Phlager stood. "What's important is to get Sanders back safely." He paused and looked closely at Liz. "We need someone to stay here in case a call comes in, and we need someone in the capital to be near Bob's phone at home and the paper.

"Miss Sanders, you would be the logical person to remain here. Mr. Creston will have someone with you all the time. If you're willing, you should call the university and tell them Professor Sanders is sick—flu or something—and you've come to stay until he gets back on his feet. Tell the same to your boss at the paper.

"Bob, you should go back. We can arrange to get your home phone and your direct line at the paper patched, so a call to one will ring on both.

"I guess I don't have to tell you both that the best chance

Sanders has is if this is kept secret. If we haven't heard anything in two or three days, a week at most, or if somebody gets wind of it, we'll decide then whether to open it up. I hope we'll have some kind of lead before then."

Both of us nodded agreement and Creston and Phlager left us alone.

I took her hand. "Liz, I hate like hell to leave you here with this."

Liz seemed calmer than she had been since last night. "I don't like it either. I want to do something." She paused. "But I guess this is what we ought to do. I can't really think of anything better.

"You know, my mother used to worry about this kind of thing when Daddy was working in New York. It never happened, but he always knew it might and finally decided it was time to stop taking the chance. I was too young to realize what was going on, but I think the two years she had with him before the cancer started were her happiest in a long time."

I decided to leave the car with Liz and asked Phlager for a ride back to the capital.

As we pulled out, Phlager turned to me in the back seat and said, "You know, Bob, this isn't likely to be an ordinary kidnapping. The real reason we're not going public is that we want to try to retrace Sanders's steps. I'm going to contact the foundation he was working for and hope they'll let us have any material he may have given them before this happened.

"He may be dead already, but if he isn't, the only way we can get him back in one piece may be to nail the people he was chasing."

"Christ, Bill, that could take months," I said.

"Or never," Phlager said.

CHAPTER 13

Not a hell of a lot was said on the ride back. Phlager did tell me that the effort to find whoever had set Kehler on Sanders wasn't starting from scratch—that the attorney general's office had been looking into the *CR&P* ownership at the request of the authorities in two of our neighbor states.

"So what have you found?" I asked.

"Well, not a gold mine. The approach in both cases was made on the basis of potential commercial code violations— unfair competition stuff. I didn't get all the details, but my understanding is that somebody claiming to represent SNS Associates had been approaching supermarkets, convenience stores, drug stores, and other establishments in the suburbs of the major cities and offering unusually high fees for space to place daily newspaper vending machines and racks—but with the proviso that they provide space to no directly competing publications. The issue was a restraint of trade question, and we were asked only for background on SNS.

"They didn't give us anything that indicated an organized crime connection and, to tell you the truth, we didn't exactly put it on the front burner. Young Bruce Touhy was given the file and from what I'm told, he hasn't developed much except a list of SNS Enterprises property holdings in the state."

"They have some other property?"

"I think so. I haven't seen the file."

"Boy, that's weird. These guys show up one day, take over

the second biggest paper in the state with money from God knows where, spend like oil sheiks, and nobody knows from nothing. Can't you get into their bank account—subpoena the company records?"

"We may do that eventually, Bob. But before this happened, the case was strictly low-level, and Markham Lee was not entranced with the idea of provoking a fight with a newspaper by poking into its books. You know, publishers are like porcupines. One nudge they interpret as unfriendly and they spear you with the First Amendment. If we had Sanders's papers, we might have something hard to go to a judge with, but even with the indication of kidnapping, the connection with the paper is hearsay. Unless we get something more, I don't know how we're going to get at Shiu and Swift and their backers. Maybe the guys in Chicago can pry something loose."

He didn't sound optimistic and we rode a while in silence. Then a nasty thought occurred to me.

"Listen, Bill, do you think these guys are going to come after Liz and me? It was my phone they tapped, and she talked to Frank about his project too. And how the hell do I deal with Swift and Shiu now?"

"Well, we've got her covered and you'll have someone close, also. I don't think Swift and Shiu are likely to blow their cover unless things really get out of hand. From what you tell me, there's no real link between them and Kehler, except through the Bright kid and that hangs on what some people would call guilt by association. I'd say, just do your job like nothing happened—but if either gives you any funny sign, let me know."

It was getting dark when we got back and I had Phlager drop me at home. The apartment, which used to be kind of cozy for one person, now was lonely. I sat at the dining table sipping a beer and tried to think of something brilliant, but all I could think of was Liz.

I called Frank's place and she answered on the second ring.

"How's it going, honey?"

"OK. You gave me a fright. You're the first to call."

I heard a mumbling in the background. "The trooper here says it would be better if we don't tie up the line, Bob. I better hang up."

Great. I watched TV for a couple of hours, finished a six-pack and went to bed. I dreamed about Swift, fretting over a headline. "Campus Mystery! Teacher Vanishes!" He shakes his head and tries again. "U Prof Does Judge Crater; Cops Baffled." Swift smiles and I wake up in a sweat.

I took a bus to work the next morning—a new experience. At least half the people with the papers had them turned to the sports page, and most of them didn't appear to like what they were reading.

Behind me, a gruff-voiced man was telling his seatmate what he thought about the story.

"It's a goddamn shame, this paper. This kid makes one mistake and they got him labeled for life. I don't like these faggots, but this sounds like the kid isn't really queer. Now he'll probably have to leave town—his family, too. Just for a goddamn cheap story. This used to be a good paper, but they been turning it into a damn scandal sheet. I'm gonna cancel my subscription today."

"Yeah," said his companion. "Me, too. Just when the high school had a team that looked like maybe it could win a state championship, these guys gotta ruin it. I don't know what's wrong with that kid, but he was sheer hell going off tackle. Why the hell don't they go looking for homos in Richfield? They got a team we would have had a hard time beating."

The bus let me off around the block from the paper, and as I turned the corner, I ran into the fringes of a crowd that had filled the sidewalk and was spilling half across the street in front of the *CR&P*.

Actually, it was several crowds. The biggest group was

high-school kids, milling around and yelling at everyone who came in and out of the building.

"Crap! Crap! This paper is crap! Clap! Clap! If you hate this paper, clap!" One knot of six boys and girls chanted— clapping hands sharply at each refrain.

In front of the building, about a dozen young guys in their twenties were picketing with hand-printed signs. "Stop Fag Bashing!" said one. "Homophobia Is What's Sick," said another.

To one side, a group of older men and women were gathered around a card table. I worked my way over to see what they were doing. "Boycott the *Register & Press*," the sign on the table said. "Cancel your subscriptions here."

I ducked down the alley and went into the paper through the composing room door. The shop was relatively quiet, and I climbed the steps to the second floor, coming out just down the hall from Swift's office.

The door was firmly closed, but I could hear Shiu. His words weren't audible, but the tone was in the red zone between rage and fury. He was walking back and forth in front of Swift's desk and gesticulating wildly. Through the window in the office wall, belt-high to people of average height, it looked like a disembodied head framed by flailing arms moving across the bottom of a TV screen.

Grace and Al Wilks were working at the copy desk and trying not to appear interested in what was going on across the room. I sat down with them and said, "Well, Stanley, this is another fine mess you've gotten us into."

Grace didn't smile. "That's been going on for half an hour. I don't think Swift has said six words."

"Yeah, but when he does it'll probably be to pin the blame on somebody else," Bicker muttered. "I'd hate to be Farley today."

Just then, Swift stood up behind his desk and waved at Shiu. His high-C voice came through the glass, but not enough to be understandable. Shiu's head disappeared, which meant he had sat down in one of the chairs in the cubicle. Swift sat down and continued to talk at a lower decibel level.

"He's just picked up the phone," Grace said. "Here comes something."

In the front of the room, the phone rang at the society desk. Mary Frasci picked it up, listened a moment, and hung up. She dug around in the wire basket on her desk and then headed for Swift's lair carrying a sheaf of papers. She looked about as happy as a suckling pig arriving at a wolves' convention.

Mary was with Swift and Shiu for about ten minutes. She came out with a relieved, dazed look on her face and walked over to Grace.

"Mr. Swift says I should tell you to save room for a three-inch box on the front page. I'll have the copy in ten minutes or so."

"About what?" Grace asked.

"About the paper sponsoring discount youth tickets for the rock concert this weekend." Mary looked smug.

"Come on, Mary, what's this about?" I said.

"Really, that's what they're going to do. I think it's supposed to take the steam out of that," she said, gesturing with her head toward the front of the building where the chanting and clapping could be heard. She went to her desk and began working on her terminal.

"A rock concert?" Bicker said. "More damn foolishness."

"Maybe not," Grace said. "It might help. I read those tickets for the concert were going for twenty-five dollars, and there might be a lot of those kids who'd appreciate a break on that."

"Bribery," Bicker said.

"You damn betcha," Grace replied. "Right down this outfit's alley."

The concert was running two full days at a place called Turg's Turf & Tree Farm about eleven miles out of town.

Turg had been defoliated with Old Testament-class infestations of gypsy moths, cinch bugs, and cutworms all in the same season a couple years back and had been trying to stay afloat by renting his acres out for touring concerts.

The old boy had been a Farm Bureau right-winger and a Jerry Falwell fundamentalist when he was growing fescue and elms, but lately had taken to reading *Rolling Stone,* driving Italian sports cars, and wearing his shirts open to the navel. He had enough gold chain around his neck to moor the Love Boat.

The next day's paper had the front page box offering concert tickets for $6.50 to high school kids who presented their student ID's at the *CR&P* classified counter. That drew an even bigger crowd of kids than the previous day, but this time they were in a relatively orderly line waiting to get into the lobby. The gays and the boycotters were still in front, but they weren't getting much attention; a couple of days later, both gave up.

I was involved in none of these festivities, but was spending my days sitting by my phone at the statehouse pressroom and my nights doing the same at home. In the middle of the second day, I called Phlager.

"Listen, this isn't going anywhere. If they were going to ask for something to return Frank, they would have contacted somebody by now," I said.

"Yeah, I was talking to Creston about it a few minutes ago. Tell you what, we'll keep our people on your phones here and Sanders's up there, but you don't need to sit by. Stay in touch . . . we may need you."

"How about Liz?"

"Well, I guess she could come back too if she wants. I'll call her," Phlager said.

I felt liberated but not a hell of a lot better. It was obvious that every day that went by without word made it worse for Frank. I waited a couple of hours and called Liz at Frank's apartment. The phone was picked up, but there was no response until I said, "Liz, Liz, are you there?" a couple of times.

Then a deep male voice answered. "Mr. Wartovsky? Miss Sanders has gone out. I'm not sure where, but she took the car that was here. Oh, and I'm sorry, but would you mind not ringing this line? It sets off the recording and tracing stuff every time." He gave me a number where I could reach Creston if I had to get through.

That made me feel worse. I didn't know if Liz was on the way back or what. I sat around the pressroom until nearly 8:00 and finally gave up and went to the Next Door.

Grace and some of the staff were there as usual. I sat down for a beer and a burger. "What's happening?" I asked.

"Well, it looks like this rock concert deal is getting real big," he said. "Swift wants pieces promoting it every day—mentioning of course that the civic-minded CR&P is helping the kids get to see it. He sent Diana Osky to Des Moines to do some pieces on the featured band that is going to be here. Doralee's totally pissed that she didn't get the assignment, although when she found out Shiu was flying Di down there, she cooled off some. She's scared stiff of that guy."

"Shiu flew Diana to Iowa? In what, the helicopter?"

"No, I think he rented a small plane so they could get back here tomorrow early. Tandee went, too. By the way, do you know when Liz is coming back? With Whine gone, we're out of luck for pictures."

The question irritated me more than it should have. "No, damn it, I don't know. I thought she was checking in with you."

"Okay, Bob. I just asked. We'll bump along."

I went home and waited to hear from Liz. Nothing. The next morning I called Creston at the number the trooper had given me.

"Where 'he hell's Liz Sanders," I demanded.

"Whoa, Bob. What's under your saddle? She's staying with a friend on campus—said it was getting her down to sit around her Dad's place. I talked to her this morning and she sounds some better. You want the number?"

"No," I snapped. "Next time you hear from her, you might tell her that if she wants to keep her job, she ought to check in with the city editor." I hung up. Doralee wasn't the only one with a case of the red ass.

I checked out the statehouse pressroom, made a quick round of the agencies, and carried a small sheaf of handouts over to the paper. "My computer's acting up," I told Grace. "I thought I'd work over here and keep from losing copy every half hour."

He nodded and I sat down at Diana's empty desk to compose some deathless prose about the number of potholes that had been repaired by the state highway department since the spring thaw, and the outbreak of swine cholera that the agriculture department had snuffed out in the western part of the state. After an hour or so, Shep Carley came over with some sheets of wire copy and said Grace had asked if I had time to put together a primary campaign story from the separate pieces on the candidates. It kept me busy until Diana and Tandee walked into the newsroom about midafternoon.

I got up from the desk, and Diana plunked her notebook and purse down. "I was just keeping your terminal warm," I said lamely.

"No problem, Bob. But I guess I better get to work. Grace wants a long piece on the band, and it took us so long to get back I'm going to be under the gun."

"Trouble flying?" I asked.

"Oh, no. It's just that we couldn't get our publisher out of there. He sat in on the interviews and developed quite a case on the lead singer. Before we left, he insisted on going into town and buying her candy and flowers. I think it's a true case of East meets West and falls apart."

"What does she look like?"

"A sight to behold," Diana said. "You have to understand this is a punk band, so what you might think constitutes feminine beauty may be somewhat out of date. So imagine a six-foot blonde with a hairdo like Harpo Marx and a safety pin through her nostril. When we were there, she was wearing what looked like a scuba diver's outfit—only in red leather. I thought Shiu was going to try to climb her like a tree before we left."

"Sounds gorgeous. What's her name?"

"She grew up as Martha Korpak, but now it's Sister Song. The band is called Post Partum Repression, and she fits right in with them. But you'll see them—they're winding up down there tonight, and Shiu arranged to have them come early and appear at the paper to meet their fans tomorrow afternoon. I hope somebody alerts the National Guard. But hey, I've got to get going on this."

I left Diana and wandered around the newsroom for a while before deciding to take an early slide. I got a few up on the rush hour at the Next Door and was tracking a bit fuzzily when Sam Darlington came in.

"Hey, Liz called in. She'll be back to work tomorrow," he said. "I guess her old man is better."

I didn't know if that meant something or not, but it didn't seem to matter as much as seeing if I could get ahead of the bartender's efforts to keep the beer cooler stocked. He won, as usual, and I lurched over to the park about midnight to get a cab home.

I wasn't very quiet when I arrived, but when I went into the bedroom, Liz was curled up and breathing steadily. She even could have been sleeping. I debated with myself whether to wake her, but couldn't think of anything coherent to say and just flopped down beside her. I remember thinking, if I snore tonight, it'll serve her right.

She was up and showered before I could even open one eye the next morning. When I finished in the bathroom, she came up and kissed me hard on the mouth before she said a word.

"Your toothpaste turns me on," she said. "Come on, coffee's ready."

"You going to tell me where you've been for the last two days? I thought maybe they got you, too."

"Come on, Bob, you knew I was all right. Mr. Creston said you called. I didn't call back because I just didn't want to talk about or even think about it all for a while. It was starting to get to me."

"So where'd you go?"

"I went to see some friends."

"Who?"

"Now wait a minute. I went to see friends from school. I've got some, you know. Kids, like me. Don't give a damn types. Like me. You wouldn't like them."

I felt like a shit and not just from the previous night's effort to create a boomlet in Stroh's stock. "Liz, I'm sorry. I was worried and I am hung over. Bear with an old man's suspicious mind."

She smiled. "You'll never have a reason to be suspicious. I'll tell you if something is happening that changes us. I'm not good at keeping secrets or telling lies."

"Enough said." I sipped the coffee and could feel life returning. It made my headache feel more real.

I dropped Liz at the paper and drove over to the statehouse. I spent the morning sucking up more coffee and trying to shut out the sound of the pressroom card game. I felt good enough by midday to go outdoors and went by the paper to see if anyone was interested in lunch.

There was a black Cadillac limousine parked in front of the building. I could tell from the plates that it was a rental job.

"We got visitors?" I asked Darlington when I got up to the newsroom.

"Not we, Shiu. He went to the airport to pick up the singer lady and gave her the grand tour of the place. Diana thinks he must have given her airfare, because the band travels by bus. They're supposed to be showing up here this afternoon."

Darlington was the cool cat on the staff, single and devoted to girl-hunting vacation expeditions to Acapulco and the Caribbean, but he was clearly impressed by Sister Song. "Boy, what a piece of work that is. The last time I saw shorts that short was in Times Square, and the last time I saw a girl that big she was a he."

"Shiu's got himself a queen?"

"No, this is a real woman. A real-big-real-woman," Darlington said with enthusiasm. "Susan Anton would cry for envy. Jayne Kennedy would hide in a closet. Brooke Shields would go home for her high heels."

"My God, where is this basketball player?"

Darlington turned back to his computer screen. "With Shiu. Upstairs, I guess."

I shopped for lunch companions and found no one. Liz was out on assignment. So I went down the block to Angelina's and sat in the front window munching a foot-long and slurping a Coke. I could see the newspaper building and in about ten minutes Shiu came out with Sister Song.

Sam hadn't been exaggerating. She was shorter than the Statue of Liberty, but better built. Shiu's head came to her belt, and if she hadn't bent from the waist to hear what he was saying as he escorted her to the car, he would have been giving a navel address.

I went back to the Capitol. Liz called late in the afternoon, and I swung by the paper to pick her up. We headed for a rib joint just outside town.

"I was working out at Turg's this afternoon," she said. "They were setting up for the concert, and I did a couple of features for tomorrow's story. We sure are giving this thing a lot of space."

"Well, you know Swift. He doesn't do anything halfway."

"I'll say. Before I went out I heard him telling Grace we were going to give the concert a full page Saturday. And a funny thing, he said, 'That ought to satisfy the little gook bastard.' It sounded like he really hates Shiu."

"Could be. Mr. Moto apparently gave him a sixteen-inch reaming on that football player story." I thought a moment.

"Maybe that's the way to break out something on Frank. I'll tell Phlager tomorrow morning."

Liz had her head down and I touched her arm. She looked up with wet eyes. "Oh, Bob, do you think anything is going to help? It's been almost a week. I just don't think . . ."

"Liz, don't give up now. He's gone, but we don't know anything else has happened. It's a long time ahead that we have to stop hoping he's all right."

To change the subject, I asked, "Were you back when the band showed up at the paper?"

"Oh, God, I was just coming back and I got caught in the middle of it. The crowd was so big they had to block the street off and when they showed up in their beat-up old bus, the kids nearly tipped it over trying to get to it."

"Did you see the singer?"

"No, she wasn't there that I could see. Rick says he heard Shiu set her up in a hotel suite and that she went back to rest after she visited the paper. He says Shiu went somewhere to rest this afternoon, too."

"Ah, the molehill travels to conquer the mountain," I said.

"Yeah," Liz said. "What is it about you short men that makes you get so horny about tall women?"

I sat up straight in the car seat. "I am not short. I may have been of medium size until Shiu arrived, but now I am tall. And anyway, women of all sizes make me horny."

"We'll see about that after dinner," Liz said.

CHAPTER 14

When I got to work Friday, there was a message to call Phlager. I have to admit I was worried about returning the call; despite what I had told Liz, I didn't expect good news.

Phlager was businesslike as usual. He acknowledged Liz's report about Swift's apparent growing dislike of Shiu without noticeable interest and launched into a report.

"Three things, Bob. First, we got a faint lead yesterday when the troopers made a second swing around with pictures of Sanders and Kehler. A gas station attendant about one hundred miles north said he thinks he may have filled their car about 2:00 A.M. the morning after Sanders was taken. But he's blank on the car—says it was dark and a big sedan. Anyway, we've fanned out from there and are trying to pick up the trail. But as you know, the country up there gets pretty sparsely populated . . . a lot more trees than people.

"Second, young Touhy came up with something that may be nothing. He was poking through the records at the airport and found that Shiu had notified the manager that he intended to use the helicopter on night flights and would be using air-traffic facilities after midnight. He also contracted for daytime maintenance on the 'copter, which I guess means they don't intend to use it during the days. I'm not sure where that fits, if at all, but it could have something to do with what Sanders told you about the helicopter being important in all this.

"Finally, we've decided that there's no point keeping quiet anymore. What we're going to do is call a press conference Saturday at the university and announce that the FBI is coming into the case. We'll make an appeal for any information from the public."

"That last isn't particularly good news, is it, Bill?"

Phlager paused. "Bob, no point in trying to kid you. Creston doesn't think we're going to get Sanders back safe. He says, and the FBI guys agree, that this looks more and more like a hit than a kidnapping. Still, there's that sighting up north. . . ."

"What shall I tell Liz? She's getting pretty low."

"What we're doing and what we've found out—not what we're thinking. Time enough for that if nothing more turns up."

At least Liz was keeping busy. Swift had assigned both her and Tandee to work the concert that night. She and Whine were going out to Turg's early, and he was supposed to come back in as soon as he had some crowd and performance shots. She was going to stay for the whole show. I had no assignment, but I decided to go out for the after-dark activities and drive Liz back when it was all over.

Diana was covering the story with help from Kirk Bright, and Doralee Green, for God's sake, was going to be in the office to take their dictation and help Grace put the story together. He said Swift planned to stay around, but didn't want to get involved in the story because rock music gave him a headache. That constituted a full-court press for our staff, but putting Doralee on the team was like starting Mickey Rooney against the Boston Celtics.

Liz called me at the Capitol in late afternoon from the farm and asked me to run by the paper to pick up a long lens she had thought Tandee would be carrying.

"This looks like it's going to be a big crowd," Liz said. "The kids have been pouring in since three o'clock and nothing is going to happen until seven. You better start early; the road already is bumper to bumper."

"A lot of cops around?" I asked.

"Come on, Bob, this isn't southern California. There's no Hell's Angels or weirdos out here. Good, milk-fed, midwestern kids. Turg has half a dozen of his neighbors dressed in rent-a-cop outfits, and there are a couple of deputies from the county around."

I went into the office about a quarter to six, found the lens, and stopped by the city desk.

"Hey, you ain't dressed right for a rock concert," Darlington said. "You show up in a suit, and they'll run you off for a narc. What you need is some cutoff jeans and a tank top. Orange, maybe."

"Don't worry, Sam, I'm going as a mid-life crisis case. I'll just go 'round staring at the teenie boppers' boobs and act like I don't know anything about the music."

"So do you?"

"Sure. I know all the words to 'Why Don't We Do It in the Road' and 'Bobby McGee.' I'll get along just fine."

"Sure you will. They'll figure you for a time traveler from the last century. Just watch out for the jail bait, buddy."

Did he mean Liz? "Is that a crack, Darlington?"

"Come on, Bobby. You know better. Besides, it's Shiu that has problems with runaway gonads."

"Oh, what now?"

"Di says he's gone totally ape over that big singer girl. He chauffeured her all around town last night and drove her out to Turg's this afternoon. He came back here and just left again carrying his flying jacket. God knows what he's up to now."

I had a bite to eat and headed out to the concert. Turg's was less than a mile from the interstate, but you had to go about five miles past it to the nearest exit and then double back on a gravel road in a state of repair that indicated old man Turg was no buddy of the county highway commissioner.

The traffic was moving at two speeds, slow and not at all, on the narrow, bumpy road. Most of the cars around me were loaded down with young people, about half appearing to be in their twenties and the rest of high-school age. It had been a very dry month, and, from more than a mile ahead as the line of traffic approached the farm, I could see a dust cloud rising over the barren field that was being used for parking.

As I got to the entrance of the field, I leaned out to talk to a teenaged kid in bib overalls directing traffic. The beat and boom of a rock band was rolling out over the farm; and the people in the cars were bobbing and weaving as they maneuvered for parking places on the crowded lot. It looked to me like there were several thousand cars and trucks already pulled into snaky rows.

I waved the cardboard press tag Grace had given me before I left the paper. "Hey, have you got some place for press parking? I've got to get out of here early."

"You can drive around to the right and park near them band buses, mister. But you still got to give me a dollar."

"For press?"

"For God, if He shows up, Mr. Turg told me. Nobody parks free."

I paid up and bumped about a quarter of a mile across an open field to the area the kid indicated. It was behind the stage, which had been built about twenty feet above the ground on steel scaffolding at the bottom of a hill where Turg's farmhouse stood. Out of force of habit, I noted a row of outdoor telephones not far from the entrance to the parking lot and patted my pants pocket to assure myself I had change.

There were three buses of varying age and condition parked well apart about fifty feet back of the stage. One, a converted school bus, was painted in the style of a Jackson Pollock drip and drizzle picture and carried the name "The Fuggers," in violent purple letters. Both of the other buses looked to be Trailways or Greyhound models from the

1960s. One carried a rather modest sign, "Baraboo," which I took to be the name of the band rather than the destination, and the other a wheels-to-roof, nose-to-tail legend in that garish orange that the FAA at one time tried to sell the airlines to enhance "see-and-be-seen" flying. "Post Partum Repression," it said.

As I pulled up beside that bus, the music from the stage ended and a roar of applause rose from the field in front of it. I couldn't see the crowd, but it sounded big indeed. As I started out of the car, I heard Shiu's voice from an open window in the bus above me. The window, in the rear of the bus, had some sort of light drapery across it, masking the interior but not muffling sound.

"That's a lovely costume, dear. But I bet you can't wear anything under it, can you?"

The response was a giggle.

"Come on, let me have a peek," Shiu said. There was the sound of movement, bumping against the side of the bus, and another giggle. "Not now, Shiggy, I've got to go on soon."

"Here," said Shiu. "Let me fill your glass. This is good champagne and it'll just lose its bubbles if we don't drink it."

"I shouldn't, Shiggy. The boys don't like it if I've been drinking before a show."

"Oh, come on, lovely lady. I bet you go on stoned plenty of the time. It'll relax you."

I stood there for a few moments and suddenly started feeling like a Peeping Tom. I grabbed the lens from the back seat of my car and walked toward a wooden snow fence that surrounded the stage. One of Turg's homemade cops looked at my tag and waved me through an opening.

There was a narrow metal staircase going up the back of the stage. Next to it, half a dozen of what appeared to be young men were lounging on folding aluminum chairs, drinking Coors and eating franchise fried chicken.

I say young men because several had their upper clothing

open to the navel and there were no signs of feminine appurtenances. Otherwise, they were dressed in a variety of multihued costumes that could have been either male or female. One chap had the remains of a full-dress tails suit with a formal bow tie around his neck but no shirt. Another wore glittering, sequined running shorts and a coat with epaulets that must once have been the proud property of a circus ringmaster. All had exceedingly long hair, but no beards or mustaches, and enough theatrical paint on their faces to cover a good-sized barn. One's face was painted black above the nose, white below. Another was all silver with a blue crosshatch overlaid. I have been in better-looking bad dreams.

"Hey, man, what you doin' back here? This's for performers."

"Press," I muttered, waving the lens and walking by rapidly.

The snow fence around the stage left walkways on each side and an open space of about twenty feet deep in front to keep the audience back. Diana and Kirk were seated at a plank table set up a few feet out from the lip of the stage. Diana had a portable typewriter in front of her. A couple of local TV crews were also on hand, set up near the fence separating the press area from the audience. Standing with one of the crews was Lew Fraser, my National Press friend from the statehouse.

"What the hell are you doing out here?" I asked Fraser. "Don't tell me NP pays overtime to cover rock concerts."

"NP pays overtime for the Second Coming or anything better. No, I'm here to listen to the music, Bob. The wire doesn't take concerts smaller than Woodstock these days, but the promoters sent us press passes anyway. On my salary, it's a welcome freebee. But you're the one I wouldn't have taken for a punker."

"Just came out to give a friend a lift," I said, looking around for Liz.

The crowd on the rolling field in front of the stage was packed tight and almost out of sight in the deepening darkness. From somewhere in the crowd, spotlights were aimed at the stage, and their beams cut through swirls of rising gray smoke. It could have been from cigarettes, but you didn't have to be a Drug Enforcement Administration pot-sniffing German shepherd to come to the conclusion that something besides your basic Winstons and Kools were being consumed.

"Christ, you could get stoned just sitting here," I said.

"Hey, man," Fraser said with a grin. "You getting the munchies, too?"

Liz appeared at my side. "What a sideshow," she said. "Am I glad you're here. Come with me to the light tower so I can take some stage shots. I need someone to cover my rear. I went out there a while ago and some creep grabbed the back of my pants when I tried to climb up to get above the crowd."

"What, one of Turg's guys?"

"Hell, no. He has his clowns at the gates and along the fences to keep out crashers. I mean one of the paying guests. They're getting a little playful."

We went out the back, circled the stage area, and worked along the snow fence to the spectator area until we found a opening guarded by a ticket-taker and a Turg trooper.

I've always believed that when you give someone a uniform and a badge it alters personality quicker than LSD, and the newer or more temporary the authority that goes with them, the more arbitrary is the wearer thereof. It was no different here. After no more than five minutes of arguing, we were permitted inside.

The audience in the area we traversed was what we newspaper types call "a youthful crowd"—mostly teenagers and the early twenties, some in their thirties, and a few men and women who got their social security numbers before me.

There also were some folks who, if you found them drinking at a bar you were entering for the first time, you would be well advised to take your custom elsewhere. The kid punkers who made up the majority of the crowd were trying to look tough; these older types didn't have to try.

The intermission between bands was still on as we worked our way to the nearest light tower about one hundred feet into the crowd. With two cameras around her neck and a canvas accessory bag dangling off her hip, Liz grabbed the steel framework and pulled herself up to a position about ten feet off the ground.

"Hey, momma, come on down and have a brew," a hairy gentleman tastefully attired in a Nazi helmet, chrome-studded leather vest, and denim cutoffs yelled. "Or, hey, I'll bring you one. Don't go 'way."

As the man approached the tower and got ready to climb, I spoke into his ear. "If you go up there, you won't be in the picture."

"What pitcher?" he said, turning toward me.

"The one she's taking for *Rolling Stone*. She's getting crowd shots for the next edition, and she told me she wanted a shot from above with you and your group in the foreground."

"No shit? In *Stone*?" The lunk let go of the tower and started back toward his pals. After about two steps, he turned and came back.

"Hey, what kind of bullshit are you trying to feed me, you old fart? How's she gonna take pictures of us and the crowd in the dark? I ain't stupid."

I smiled. "Infrared, hyperstrobe, laser-augmented flash bulbs," I said. "New development."

King Kong scurried off just as the next band, Baraboo, arrived on stage. The crowd applause swelled as they launched into what appeared to be more an attempt to destroy their instruments, with desperate pounding of drumheads and keys and snatching at strings, than make music. Liz got several shots and climbed down.

"I suppose I better come back when Post Partum comes on," she said. "I imagine our publisher has promised them nothing less than a front page picture."

"Good," I said. "I'll bring a camera too, and we'll have some good shots of you being gang-banged to go with them. Meanwhile, let's get the hell out of here."

We worked our way back to the press area as Baraboo's first so-called song ended. Next came what I recognized as music—a medley of familiar circus themes, and I leaned over to Diana to ask guidance—when the band suddenly changed the beat and the melody into a rock-and-roll rendition so crashing that I thought the boards of the stage above us would shortly start popping their knots.

Diana could see I was puzzled. "It's their signature," she shouted into my ear. "'Bozo's March,' they call it. It was their first big hit."

I stepped into the open space in front of the stage scaffolding and took a good look at the band. It was the group I had seen when I arrived and all had added cheery red clown noses to their previous getups.

"Clowns?" I asked after sitting down again.

"That's the Baraboo connection," Diana said. "That's where the Ringling Brothers started out in Wisconsin. It's their shtick—they have a whole album of circus songs. Wait till they play 'Do It to Me on the Flying Trapeze.'"

I shook my head which made it hurt even more. "Boy, I sure must have missed something."

Liz smiled. "Just the last ten years."

It took a full forty minutes for Baraboo to run through its repertoire and exhaust itself. After the last rivet-popping, metal-fatiguing number ended, the band made its way down the back stairs, makeup streaked with sweat, and the members stretched out on the grass behind the stage. The audience on the field in front was humming and buzzing like a power station with an occasional shriek of joy or pain—hard to tell which—cutting through the undertone.

"Post Partum's up next," Liz said. "You'll like them better. I've heard them even do some oldies and goldies.

"Listen, I'm going to try the stage for some level shots."

She left, but was back in a few minutes. "Got all the way up to the top of the steps, but the old man up there wouldn't let me on the stage."

"Tall guy with a fringe of white hair?" I asked. Liz nodded.

"That sounds like Turg. I met him once at a Senate Agriculture Committee hearing. He was trying to get a state tax depreciation allowance on commercial turf. Maybe I can talk him into letting you up."

We climbed the stairs and I got lucky. Turg remembered me.

"Sure, I 'member you from the Capitol. You're the only one who even asked me to explain what kind problems a turf farmer got. Did a fair story too, I recollect. Of course, them crooks over there wouldn't pass my bill.

"What the hell you doin' out here in this madhouse? My God, if Momma had lived to see what the home place she and Paw worked over had come to, she'd die. Trampling the grass, throwing beer cans all over . . . shit, I even find girls' underwear out there next day," he said, waving at the crowd.

Turg was willing to let me and Liz on the stage, but warned us to stay out of sight behind the huge sound amplifiers.

"Band won't stand for anybody on the stage when they come on. I guess they won't care though if she takes a couple pitchers once they get started. But then you both go back down, hear?"

We stationed ourselves behind the equipment and after five minutes the four male members of Post Partum Repression, dressed in denim pants and shiny red shirts piped with white, came up to the stage. They were by far the most conservatively outfitted of the groups if you discounted the effect of the safety pin each member had thrust through his left nostril.

They noodled a few minutes with their instruments and launched into their opening number, an adaptation of "Danny Boy" that probably would have united Ireland in a spontaneous outbreak of ethnic outrage.

The applause was just dying down when a high-pitched scream came from behind the stage. The band didn't appear to notice, but Liz and I turned to see two figures scrambling up the stairs.

In the lead, bent in exertion, was a lean, light figure. As we looked down, the ringlets of blonde hair whipped about like a dust mop being shaken out a window as arms and legs pumped up the stairs. Halfway to the top, the head went back and another shriek cut through the sound of the band just starting its second number.

There was a second figure about a dozen steps behind the first. The weak light of the stage glowed dimly off a round white globe, which appeared from our vantage to be set atop a dark, soft-textured lump heaving up the stairs.

The band heard the second scream, and the players turned toward the stairway. Liz and I stepped in back of the speakers as a tall young woman reached the top step, stumbled as she reached level footing, and lurched to the front of the stage.

Sister Song was dressed in one knee-high red boot. The rest of what appeared in the full glare of the big spotlights was all Sister Song, nearly six feet of gleaming white skin and a mop of wildly disarranged and, as then could be seen by all, bleached-blonde hair.

Behind her at the top of the stairs was her pursuer, that distinguished pillar of American journalism and exemplar of Asian aviation, Shigetsu Shiu. His costume was only slightly more complete, consisting of a well-worn leather flight jacket, topped by a gleaming white impact plastic motorcyclist's helmet. Red lightning bolts shot down each side of the bubble-shaped helmet, and a smoked plastic visor was pushed up above the forehead. From beneath the sheepskin fringe of the jacket, white shirt tails protruded like a ballet dancer's tutu, and below them, Shiu was as bare-assed as the object of his chase.

It was like a freeze-frame photograph; the band members caught with their hands on their instruments and their heads pivoted toward the rear of the stage.

The crowd went dead silent as Sister Song stood wavering slightly from side to side in the crossed spotlights—her mouth working silently and her eyes swinging wildly around the stage. Next to me, I could hear Liz clicking away, but I could not blink, let alone move. Somewhere in the back of the brain where the Id keeps its files, I recall taking note, "Awfully small tits for such a big broad."

Sister Song took a step forward and turned to face the band—her hands fluttering. The movement put her next to one of the band's microphones and her words boomed out over the crowd.

"The little son of a bitch tried to rape me!"

Several band members started as if they had been jolted by simultaneous short circuits from their own electrified instruments. The bass player moved first, reaching down for the big fiddle case that had been lying next to him, opening it and trying to screen the singer from the audience. It reached only to the middle of her chest, and the drummer pulled off his shirt and tried to throw it over her shoulders from his perch above the band.

"No," she shouted, again sending her voice out over the crowd. "Leave me alone. Get that little bastard!"

Attention turned to the back of the stage, where Shiu had been standing pants-less and open-mouthed.

"Get him!" the keyboardist yelled.

"Grab the sumbitch!" the guitarist shouted.

As the band members extricated themselves from their equipment, a few titters of laughter came up from the crowd. Someone shouted, "Go, Posties, go!" and someone else, "More! More!" A slow wave of applause began in the audience as the impression grew that it was being treated to a new wrinkle of punk rock showmanship.

As the band members started toward the stairs, Sister Song plopped down on the stage and began sobbing. Liz left the concealment of the speakers to bend over her, and I moved to the railing along the back of the stage.

Shiu was scuttling down the stairs pursued by three of the bandsmen. Coming up the steps were four of the clown-costumed Baraboos, followed by a Turg rent-a-cop and a broad-hatted deputy sheriff.

Shiu saw that he was cut off and climbed over the staircase railing about halfway down and onto the struts of the stage scaffolding. He shucked off the bulky jacket and began worming through the metal web of supports to get out of reach. One of the Post Partum band members tried to follow him, but lost his footing, dangling about ten feet above the ground. Another bandsman hooked his leg over the stair railing and tried to grab the flailing legs. He got kicked in the head for his pains.

The deputy backtracked down the stairs and tried to get below Shiu, but he could not get through the maze of scaffolding. Another deputy on the ground at the rear of the stage brought the beam of an eight-cell flashlight to bear on Shiu, as he hunkered down among the supports, and the little Oriental began trying to dodge the light.

I started down the stairs to get a better view of the proceedings. The deputy, who had gotten hung up trying to crawl into the scaffolding, now had his flashlight out and with his partner on the ground was zeroing in on Shiu as he scuttled back and forth.

"Th' fuck is it, a chimp?" the lawman on the ground yelled.

"No," the officer on the stair replied. "A midget . . . a dwarf or something. I dunno . . . the big singer says he tried to hose her."

"Rape?" the first deputy said. He unbuttoned his holster and pulled out his revolver. "OK, you in there. Enough hide and seek. Come out of there or I'll blow you out," he shouted at Shiu.

I ran down the rest of the steps. The crowd, at least in the front dozen or so rows, could see that what was happening was not part of the show, and some of the spectators were getting caught up in the chase.

"There he goes behind that center support," someone yelled.

"Go in after him," someone else advised the cops.

Diana and Kirk were standing at the press table, straining to see what was happening in the scaffolding. One of the TV crews turned on its lights and between them and the deputies' flashlights, Shiu was finding it difficult to hide.

The cop with the gun now steadied it on one of the scaffold supports and yelled, "Last chance. Come out or I fire!"

"Jesus, Fred, don't shoot toward the crowd," the other deputy said.

Fred stood back and fired a shot into the air. "The next one comes in there," he yelled at Shiu.

Shiu gave a squeal of fright and clambered toward the front of the stage, finally reaching the edge of the scaffold. As he hung over the ten-foot drop, he turned to see the deputy, illuminated by the TV lights, leveling the gun. Shiu leaped off the scaffold, landing on both feet on the press table, which collapsed with a wrenching crack.

Diana, Kirk, and Fraser jumped back to avoid the splintered table and its contents. Now two TV crews were in action, and as they backtracked to try to get their cameras on Shiu, their lights flashed wildly around—compounding the confusion.

Like a paratrooper hitting the ground, Shiu rolled away from the table, jumped to his feet, wildly looked about and took off for the walkway. He bumped against me as he ran toward the rear of the stage, then shot past the deputy with the gun and the bandsmen between him and the exit.

Up on the stage, Liz and Sister Song were watching over the edge and when Shiu landed on the table, the singer screamed, "He's getting away! Grab him!"

The spectators in the front rows took up the cry. "There he goes. Stop him!" someone shouted. "Rapist! Get him!" a man bellowed. The crowd began pushing forward.

The flimsy slat fence separating the crowd from the stage bellied in, cracked, and slapped to the ground. In a moment, the entire area was filled with pushing, shoving, and yelling spectators, some trying to chase Shiu and others just trying to get out of the way. In the middle and rear of the audience, people could be heard shouting, "What's wrong? What's happening?" and suddenly the whole hillside seemed to be heaving and seething, like a lake hit by a wind squall.

I pulled myself up on the first cross support of the scaffold and above the crowd saw Shiu's white helmet bobbing among the cops and other pursuers at the rear of the stage. Then it disappeared into the dark.

As the deputies, the band members, the audience, and the TV crews floundered around the buses and cars in the field back of the stage area, I caught what might have been a gleam of the helmet again at the rise of a hill about fifty yards back.

The stage was surrounded by people trying to go in different directions. I tried to find a deputy to tell him that I thought Shiu might have taken off over the hill, but after a few minutes saw it was fruitless and pushed my way back to the press area. I found Diana and Kirk trying to retrieve the typewriter and the papers that had been scattered by Shiu's descent and trampled by the audience breakout.

"Christ's sake, forget that," I said. "Bright, get your ass down to those phones at the entrance and call Grace. Tell him we've got a big-ass story out here and hold the phone open." Kirk, wide-eyed, nodded and began pushing his way toward the phones.

I turned to Diana. "I've got what happened up top, so I

can dictate the lead. But the story will need stuff like the crowd size and the background on the concert, and I need a fill from you on that. We also need stuff from the cops and from Turg, so try to get that and bring it down to the phones."

Diana responded like a veteran. Leafing through her notebook, she quickly gave me the information I needed for a halfway coherent story and then headed toward the rear area where the crowd was still milling around looking for Shiu.

I started for the phones. I noticed in the parking field that a number of people had given up on the concert and were starting toward their cars. I was about halfway between the stage and the row of telephones, stumbling in the dim light, when a motor sound that definitely did not come from a car began just over the hill beyond the stage. It swelled, a roaring interspersed with an accelerating clacking sound, and as I looked toward the source, a massive shape rose over the ridge line.

Because I could make the connection between Shiu and the *CR&P*'s helicopter, I knew immediately what was ascending over the farm. But to the spooked, pot-befuddled crowd milling around below, the machine was a frightening apparition, and new yells and screams rose from the area of the stage and the hillside in front.

The dark shape lumbered upward to clear the hill, and a line of blinking red and blue lights went on along its huge length. At an altitude of about fifty feet, the 'copter began moving slowly forward toward the concert grounds, passing over the stage. The microphones had been left open and suddenly the engine sound was amplified to a thunderous level. That did it; the helicopter picked up speed and roared off into the night, but behind it was a mob in total panic.

I could hear cars smashing into each other in the parking area, and behind me a motor was kicked to life. I looked back to see the Fuggers' garish bus jerking to a start and heading toward the entrance. I was only about thirty feet from the telephones, where Kirk Bright had his head bent inside one of the three-sided enclosures—with the receiver to his ear.

The Fuggers' bus, gaining speed as it passed me, hit a rut and lurched to the left, heading directly for the telephone bank.

I shouted, "Look out, Kirk!" and saw the young reporter jump back reflexively as the bus crunched into the row of telephones, snapping off the metal standards just above the ground. The bus rolled on about twenty feet and stopped.

Kirk stood where the phone bank had been, staring alternately at the bus, the telephone receiver, and its dangling cord. It was neatly amputated at the point where the cord had been attached to the box.

"You OK?" I asked as I ran the last few feet.

Bright looked stricken. "Oh my gosh, Mr. Wartovsky, what are we going to do now? That was my last fifteen cents."

CHAPTER 15

The crowd was in full flight as I guided the stunned Kirk back toward the stage. The fences all around the concert grounds had been trampled down as the audience stampeded toward the parking field. We fought our way back to the rear of the stage, where we found Diana talking with a deputy in one of the sheriff's squad cars, and Liz was sitting above the crowd on the stairs.

The Baraboo and Post Partum Repression buses were still parked behind the stage. Sister Song, wrapped in a blanket and looking calmer, was sitting on a chair next to her band's bus with a deputy, notebook in hand, squatted down, and the musicians clustered around her. A couple of Turg's guards were trying to keep wandering members of the audience away from the buses. The old man himself was sitting on the ground, holding a bloody handkerchief to the side of his head.

Diana came over to us. "They're calling for ambulances and more police. There's some people hurt out there," she said, waving to the rapidly emptying hillside where the audience had been.

"I've been trying to talk to the deputies, but I think they're panicked worse than the crowd. . . . I just heard that deputy say on the radio that it was all started by a naked little man in a space helmet who got away in some kind of flying cigar. He keeps referring to the singer as 'the Sister.'"

In the hope that I could work a trade with the cops—give

them some needed information and get them to pass a message to the paper—I walked over to the squad car and tapped the deputy on the arm.

I knew some of the sheriff's older people, but not this one, a young deputy with one of those bristle brush mustaches they seem to issue with badges and guns these days. "Hey, pal, I know who that was under the stage and what he flew off in."

The deputy looked up with an annoyed expression from the microphone he had been talking into. "Step back, mister. I'm busy right here. If you've got a statement, wait by the car, and as soon as we've got some help someone will take it."

"But I can identify . . ."

He swung his legs out of the car. "Back, buddy. I'm not too busy to arrest you for interfering with an officer. You'll have a chance to tell your story."

The story. We had to do something quick about that. The paper's first copy deadline was less than ninety minutes away.

I walked back to Diana and Kirk, who was looking like a shipwreck survivor.

"Did you get through to the paper before the bus hit the phones?"

He still had the severed phone receiver in his hand. He looked at it and said, "I talked to Mr. Grace and told him there was a big story here. He put me on to Doralee, and I just had time to tell her that there had been some sort of sex crime and that the crowd was starting to panic when . . ." He waved the useless receiver.

"Jesus," I said to Diana, "they must be going nuts down there. What about the TV people? Are they going live from here?"

Diana shook her head. "I saw them arrive . . . both came in station wagons, not remote vans. I guess they were just taping."

"Well, we've got to find a phone or someway to call in," I said.

Liz had come down from the stairs and tugged at my arm, pointing up the hill at the farmhouse. "How about there?"

The three of us trudged up the hill and as we approached the house, one of Turg's uniformed guards came out on the rickety porch. He was carrying a double-barreled shotgun.

"Stop right there, folks."

"We're reporters," I said. "We've got to use the phone."

"Or you're after the gate receipts," he said. "Use the pay phones down by the entrance."

"They got knocked out," I said. "Listen, let me in. Turg's my friend, and I know he would say it was all right."

"May-be, but Mr. Turg's my boss, and I know he said don't let anybody near this house without his personal say-so. You better get."

"Turg got hurt. He's down by the stage." I started toward the porch, reaching toward my back pocket for my wallet and press pass. The guard raised the shotgun to a point over my head and pulled one of the triggers. The blast left my ears ringing and my resolve shaken. I led the way back down the hill with as much dignity as I could summon up.

We returned to my car and looked out over the road leading to the farm. It was bumper-to-bumper, and we could see some cars already had run into the ditch trying to slip past the inching line. It was obvious that there was no quick way out. In the distance, probably on the interstate, we could hear approaching sirens, which meant the mess on the county road was going to get a lot worse when they tried to get through to Turg's.

"Now what?" Liz asked.

"Maybe there's a back way out," Diana offered. "I looked on the county highway map in the office before we came out here, and I think I remember another road connecting with this one about a mile farther down. It ought to get us back towards town."

I thought about that for a moment. "I don't know. Lots of these country roads just dead end at the last farm. Then we'd be worse off. What we need most is a working phone and a quick way into town. The interstate is only a mile or so from here and maybe we'd do better heading for it and trying to hitch a ride."

We finally decided to split up; Diana and Kirk trying the back roads in his car, and Liz and I setting off across the fields toward the interstate.

I shouldered the camera bag and we hunkered under a barbed wire fence into a fairly level field. It was dark, but there was some moonlight and the footing was good.

"Did you get good photos?" I asked Liz as we trudged along.

"With that light, who knows," she said. "I'm pretty sure the shots of the singer on the stage will be good, but I'm not sure I want to give them to Swift even if we get to town on time. He'll probably headline them something like 'Rock Star Gets Down to Bare Essentials.'"

Little did we know.

"Did you talk to her at all?" I asked. "She looked hysterical."

"Mad as hell, but not hysterical," Liz said. "That's a pretty tough lady. She told me she figured on playing Shiu for the flowers and limo rides and all and put him off with a promise of some fun after the concert—when the band was planning to take off right after their last set.

"But she said he kept getting more and more insistent in the little dressing room on the bus and when she went out to check on her first number, she came back to find him taking his pants off. She told him no way and said Shiu got hot and said no bimbo was going to prick tease him and went for her costume. He got her stripped before she could whack him in the crotch with a knee and run for the stage."

"No rape?"

Liz stopped and looked at me. "I don't know if anything

else happened, but it for damn sure was assault and attempted rape. What do you think—there has to be a baby born for it to be rape?"

"No, I didn't mean that. I just wondered if it was physically possible in this case." The picture of a mouse trying to mount a giraffe had flashed through my mind. But I could see Liz was angry. "Hey, don't get me wrong—I think the little bastard ought to go to jail for tonight's performance."

"That's right, Bob. And this didn't have anything to do with sex. He was trying to humiliate her . . . hurt her physically . . . and no matter what kind of games she was into with him, it doesn't justify what he did."

We walked in silence for a while. Then I suddenly remembered the earlier call from Phlager. It wasn't the most propitious time to bring it up, but what would be. I told Liz what he had said.

"Oh, God, that means they're giving up."

"No, Liz. That just means they're opening it up to people who may have seen something and didn't know what it was. Tips from the public break a lot of cases, and it could be the difference in this one."

"I hope so. But it's been so long. Bob, do you think he's alive?"

"Liz, I don't think he is dead. I admit we haven't had any good news, but we haven't had any bad news either since that night, and I'm simply not going to give up hope."

We had reached the edge of the first field and had to climb a stone wall to get into the next. It was an entirely different story—recently plowed and with rolling terrain that made it hard to keep walking a straight line in the dark. Stumbling over furrows, sinking into freshly turned dirt and tripping over clods and rocks, we struggled along saying little.

I knew we were headed right because we could still hear sirens ahead of us and, from time to time, see a faint glow that should have been traffic moving on the interstate. Then we came to a dense clump of trees, which we should have tried to circle, but I felt we ought to keep moving on a straight course.

What we couldn't see in the grove were the low-hanging limbs that made movement slow, dangerous, and disorienting. Liz hit her head on a branch within minutes as we entered the trees, and I tripped several times—once going full length on the ground over deadfalls. I looked at my watch and realized it had been forty minutes since we left Turg's.

Next, we came to an obstacle we did have to go around—a stream that looked to be shallow but was at least twenty feet wide. Liz handed me her camera, took off her shoes, tied the laces together, hung them around her neck, and started wading into the creek.

"Oh," she said, "it's slippery . . . and, oops, getting deeper." On the bank, I saw her slide forward and then slip under the water. I dropped the camera and the bag in the high grass on the bank and waded in. She came up spitting water and I grabbed her, fighting the muck underfoot for traction. We both went down into the water. Back on our feet, soaked through, we slid and slipped back to the bank and sat on a horizontal log.

"Jesus, what a mess," Liz said.

"Well, maybe this wasn't such a good idea," I said, stripping off my shoes and pouring water out of them. I stood up and my suit streamed water. Liz, whose jeans and cotton shirt were plastered to her body, laughed, and shook water out of her hair.

"Compared to the inaugural trip of the *Titanic*, it was a terrific idea," she said. "Well, at least we'll look like we've been through a riot when we get back."

We retrieved the camera and the bag after a search and walked along the bank of the creek several hundred yards. There, of course, was a wooden bridge.

"It doesn't look safe," I said.

"Afraid you'll get wet?" Liz asked, starting across. The decrepit bridge held her, and I followed, carrying the photo equipment. We clambered up the bank and there, only a few hundred yards distant, was the big four-lane highway.

Naturally, it had a chain link fence to keep farm animals and people from wandering onto the road. Liz dug her toes into the metal lattice and got over with not much trouble, but it took three tries and some tugging by Liz from the top to get me up and over. I sat on the ground, feeling fully my age plus Liz's. But at last we were on the road.

My watch was still working and showed it had been nearly an hour and a half since we started. The normal copy deadline was gone, but I knew there was still twenty minutes or so to get at least something short into the first edition. I figured we were a minimun of eight miles from the edge of town.

Traffic was heavy but moving fast on the highway. We saw half a dozen cars and trucks carrying people who looked like they might have been at the concert, and two ambulances screamed down the left lane toward town in the first five minutes we stood on the shoulder.

At first, we tried just lifting our thumbs, but no one even slowed. Then we tried waving—I peeled off my wet coat, but it was too dark and too soaked to make much of a flag— and then shouting "Stop!" and "Help!" as well. The cars kept roaring by.

"Wait, give me the bag," Liz said. "I think I know how to get their attention." She dug into the main compartment and pulled out the strobe light flash. As the next cluster of cars approached us, she aimed the apparatus diagonally across the road and fired it several times.

One of the cars slowed and a woman, dressed in a psychedelic tee shirt and wild punker hairdo that made her look like a cartoon character who has just stuck a finger into a light socket, gaped out at us.

"Ooo, they're weird-looking," she shrilled at the driver. The car pulled away with a screech.

Another car pulled up and a bald-headed man leaned across from the driver's side.

"Jump in, honey," he said to Liz. We both started toward the car and the man barked at me, "Not you, turkey. If the lady wants a ride, she's welcome. You aren't."

Liz smiled at the big man. "Thanks, mister. I can guess what I'm welcome for. Stick your ride."

The traffic was getting heavier, but our luck didn't seem to be. Liz tried the strobe light trick again and a helmeted motorcyclist pulled over on the shoulder.

"Another lover?" I said.

The cyclist answered by taking off the helmet and letting her long red hair fall over her shoulders. "Trouble?" she asked.

"God, yes," Liz said. "We need to get to town quick."

"Well, I can take one of you. You can send somebody back for the other."

There was no doubt who would go. I wasn't about to leave Liz alone on that road, and besides, I wasn't sure I wanted my first ride on the back of a motorcycle. Furthermore, someone would have to process her photos, and there was no assurance that Whine would still be in the office.

Liz climbed on the back of the bike, pulling on the extra helmet that had been strapped to the seat.

"Tell Grace I'll be in as quick as I can, but if someone can come out in a car it might be faster. Oh, and Liz, be sure he knows it was Shiu out there," I said.

I started walking along the shoulder toward town, waving at cars as they came up behind me. No dice. I tried using the strobe, but we apparently had run the battery down or else dripped water into it from our soaked clothes.

After about a mile and another thirty minutes of slogging, I came to a lighted interchange and trudged up the off-ramp. It was still country, and I wasted another twenty minutes or so walking each way on the road looking without success for a gas station, a store, or an outdoor phone.

I started back down to the highway on the entrance ramp and heard a wheezing motor behind me. It was an aged pickup truck, which slowed and stopped in response to my frantic waving.

"I've got to get to town," I told the white-haired man behind the wheel. "I'll give you twenty bucks for a ride to the newspaper office downtown."

"You a reporter?" the old fellow asked. "Hop in."

In all, it was about ten miles to the office, and it took us about twenty minutes as he nursed the truck along at a sedate thirty.

But time goes fast when you're having fun; the old boy asked me how I got stuck on the road in wet clothes and, before waiting for an answer, treated me to a rapid-fire recitation of the sins of the media. He culminated with the statement that it was all the fault of the international-banking, communist-Iranian-Jews, who were using the money from our gasoline to buy up the papers and television stations in order to sap our moral fiber with pornography, health-food craziness, and gun control propaganda. Shooting was too good for them, he announced.

He delivered me to the front door of *The Capital Register & Press* just after 11:30. When I offered him a soggy twenty-dollar bill, the old man waved it off. "Oh, shoot no, son. 't wouldn't be the Christian thing to take money for helping a traveler in distress."

I could hear the presses rumbling as I walked around the side of the building to the night door. I squished up the stairs to the newsroom, which was dark except for one big light fixture over the city desk and a dimmer light in Swift's office.

Grace and Darlington were at the desk. A fifth of Jim Beam, Grace's "end-of-the-world" bottle (brought out of the drawer only after the desk had worked through big disasters, such as when the Democrats won a state election), was on the desk between them.

Sam's eyes widened as I approached. "Jesus, you look like the survivor of a sewer cave-in. Did Claggett find you?"

I plopped down in one of the high-tech, ergonomic chairs, probably ruining the upholstery, and accepted a Dixie cup of bourbon. "Did Liz get here all right?"

"Oh sure," Grace said. "That's how we knew to send Drew out looking for you on the interstate. Liz took her pictures in to process them, but she was shivering so I told Tandee to stay on and sent her home in a cab. You two really go in for strenuous frolics, don't you?"

I ignored the crack. "She told you what happened?"

"Yeah, and just in time. I don't think I could have made Swift stop the first edition if she hadn't come in when she did. Diana finally found a phone at some farm way the hell and gone in the country just after Liz arrived, and we were able to make some sense out of it. Anyway, we're rolling with the correct story now." Grace handed me me a front page dummy. The two big heads read:

ROCK 'N RIOT
AT CONCERT

TEN HURT AT
TURG'S FARM

In smaller type near the bottom of the page was:

Publisher Sought for
Incident with Singer

Inside was a relatively sober if sketchy account of what had happened. Inasmuch as four staff members had seen him at the concert, the article seemed to me to be excessively careful about the identification of Shiu, but otherwise it had the essential facts straight. Liz had provided a shot of Sister Song wrapped in a blanket, and one good picture of the crowd milling around behind the stage. Naturally, I wondered what had happened to the nude shots of the singer.

"Looks OK to me," I said. "Christ, I was worried with all of the wild stuff that was going around out at Turg's."

Grace looked pained. "Well, I'm afraid we went out at first with some of it. It's just that we had to work with what Bright phoned in and the wild first radio reports from the country cops. I don't blame Swift too much."

"For what, goddamm it?"

Darlington picked up a copy of the paper off the desk and turned the front page to me. One three-line headline filled it:

DWARF RAPES NUN; FLEES IN UFO!

"Oh, my God!" I cried. "Where in hell did you get that?"

"Well, the headline was Swift's, and he was so excited about it, I got to admit it seemed plausible after a while. Listen, we had to use what we had. Bright said there had been a sex crime there, and we picked up the rest on the scanner from the first police transmissions."

"The cops? You're blaming them for this abortion?"

"Cool down, damn it," Grace said. He turned to his computer terminal and keyed in several commands. "OK, come around here and look at the notes Doralee got off the police radio."

I got up and looked at Grace's screen.

"notes-green," it said in the lower case typing used to take notes hastily.

"9:35p. deputy borishoff (?) reports a 'disruption' at
turg's farm, county road 16 . . . says a woman identified
tentatively as a sister????? (unintelligible) interrupted rock concert with appearance on stage claiming rape by unnamed person.

"9:39. deputy says officers attempting to apprehend
suspect—'midget or dwarf'—in stage area . . . reports
discharge of gun fire.

"9:41. deputy james reports 'subject escaped stage'
being pursued on concert grounds. says some disorder
breaking out.

"(transmission drowned out by roaring sound) deputy reports some sort of aircraft buzzed stage area . . .
says appeared to be cigar-shaped with pulsating lights
. . . unable to identify.

"dispatcher asks james to repeat aircraft type. james
yells, 'unidentified, dammit! it's something that flies,
but i don't know what! long, like a pencil or a rocket
flying sideways.'

"9:46. deputy reports crowd out of control of officers on scene. requests assistance . . . (muffled
voices) . . . says some injuries in audience area, asks
dispatch of medical aid."

I looked up from the screen. "This is what you went with?
Jesus, Bill, you knew you had reporters out there."

"Sure, and what little we got from Bright didn't conflict all
that much. I called the phone company supervisor right
after he went off and asked for the pay phone number at the
farm, and he told me all six lines had just gone out of service.

"Besides, there was no stopping Swift once he looked at
what we were getting. He didn't pay much attention to the
story except to OK the layout, and I think was getting ready
to leave when Doralee started yelling about the call from
Bright. Then he got interested, and when we started picking
up the transmissions on the radio he stood back of Doralee
watching her notes. I guess it was that business about the

unidentified aircraft that set him off . . . he suddenly gave the damndest shriek and grabbed a blank dummy and scribbled out that head," Grace said, pointing to the paper.

"Yeah," Darlington said. "The man looked . . . well, like carried away. Like one of those people that get crazy at holy roller church services. He looked at me and yelled, 'This is it! My God, this is it! I knew it would come . . . I knew it!'"

"I argued with him that what we had was thin, but he wouldn't listen. Told me we were going to go with the story if he had to fire all of us and put out the paper himself. He was just wild-eyed," Grace said.

"But it's stupid," I said. "You guys knew the singer was called 'Sister Song' and that Shiu was sniffing after her. Didn't anyone even guess what happened?"

"Sure, Bob, but I'm telling you that Swift went completely off the deep end. I said to him, '*Sister* doesn't mean it was a nun,' and he yelled, 'Sister IS a nun, you twit! Are you telling me the plain meaning of the English language?' I thought the guy was going to go for me, for God's sake. I just gave up.

"So we went with it his way, and I guess a couple thousand papers ran before Liz came in and started telling us what really happened. I called the pressroom to stop, and I swear Swift was about to can me right then when Doralee said that Diana was on the phone.

"That did it. Swift talked to her a couple of minutes, and I could see him sag like a sandbag that just had its bottom cut out. Then he told Doralee to go back on and, I swear, there were tears in his eyes when he told me to call circulation to hold up the papers that had run."

"What then?" I asked.

Darlington turned his head toward Swift's office. "He told Bill to pull the story and go with what Diana and Liz had. Then he went back there—looking like somebody who just saw their kid run over by a truck. I guess he's still there."

I stood up. "I better talk to him. If the cops got Shiu's

identification from the singer, they're going to be coming down here soon to look for him. Swift's going to have to talk to them."

"Good luck," Grace said, downing the remaining booze in his cup. "We haven't seen or heard anything for most of an hour."

I navigated the desks back to Swift's office and looked through his window overlooking the city room. A gooseneck lamp was shining on a copy of the paper with the original headline on the desk. Behind it, Swift slumped in his chair, staring at the paper.

I opened the door quietly and went around to the front of the desk. He looked up at me blankly.

"Mr. Swift, excuse me, but I think you better start thinking about what we should tell the police if they come here looking for Mr. Shiu."

Swift smiled brightly. "Did you see it? The perfect headline!"

"But it was wrong, Mr. Swift," I said. "It was a phony."

Swift looked down. "Can't be . . . had to be true. Once in my life why couldn't it be true?" He smiled again. "Doesn't matter really, does it, old man? I've got it right here. The ultimate headline and Granville Swift wrote it."

"Mr. Swift, how about Shiu?"

The big man giggled like a little girl. "Shiu, Shiu, Shiu. Ran away, ran away. Shiu ran away, Shiu went shoo. Shoo, shoo, shoo."

"Where, Swift? Where would Shiu go?"

Swift clapped his hands, consumed by amusement. "Went to the animal fair . . . birds and beasts were there . . . the monkey got drunk . . ." He began muttering and smoothing the paper on the desk in front of him. "Wha' become of the monk?" he said, gazing at me with wet eyes.

Grace came over to the open door, glancing apprehensively at Swift.

"Bob," he said in a quiet voice. "The cops just called. They're downstairs."

CHAPTER 16

There were at least two carloads of police and they wanted to question everyone who had seen Shiu that day, so—with a detective listening—I called Liz at home. She was awake, and she said, getting ready to call the office to find out if they had heard from me, when I called.

She offered to come down to the office and a police car was sent to get her. Doralee, called by Grace, turned down a squad car ride. She said her boyfriend would drive her to the office as soon as they finished . . . ah, washing the dishes from their late dinner. A call was dispatched through the sheriff's radio to look out for Diana and Kirk on the interstate and back roads and give them an escort to town.

I had the longest story to tell, and by the time the two detectives finished with me, the other cops had taken statements from Grace and Darlington and were talking to Liz and Doralee.

I told the ranking cop, a Lt. Bardanty, about Swift's behavior earlier and suggested the man needed medical attention. To my surprise, rather than barging in and questioning Swift, he assigned one of the plainclothesmen to sit outside the managing editor's office to watch him, but keep everyone away until a psychiatrist could be found to examine him. Swift had lapsed into some kind of trance, rocking in his chair, and mumbling what sounded like nursery rhymes.

The lieutenant was not happy, however, about my suggestion that he call Creston and Phlager.

"What the hell have they got to do with this?" he asked. "This isn't a state case so far as I can see."

He knew about the Sanders disappearance, but didn't see, or didn't want to see, any connection. To tell the truth, neither did I for sure, but I figured anything to do with either Shiu or Swift might be important.

It's always amazing to see how the bureaucratic mind works. He finally agreed to put a call in to Creston when I asked him how it would go down with his chief if this did turn out to be material for the other case, and he had missed the chance to put the department in the position of supplying the key information.

It was nearly 2:00 A.M. when the resident shrink from the hospital emergency room showed up to look at Swift. Grace and Darlington had put the paper to bed and left; Doralee and her hunk had gone home to finish the dishes, and Liz and I were just waiting for a cab when Phlager, looking sleepy, but wearing his lawyer clothes, shirt, tie, and three-piece suit, came in with a state trooper.

He nodded to us and spoke briefly with Bardanty. They motioned to the pyschiatrist, who came out of Swift's office shaking his head. He spoke to Bardanty, who picked up a telephone and made a brief call. The shrink went back to the office and, with the help of the detective who had been waiting outside the door, gently raised Swift out of his chair and began walking him toward the elevator.

Phlager came over. "The doctor says there's no point in even trying to talk to him. He's taking him to the hospital and says it may be days or even weeks before Swift is lucid enough to talk to anyone. He says the man appears to have had some sort of shock that regressed him to childhood, and if we put any more stress on him he might go even deeper."

"Oh boy," I said, "I hope I didn't make it worse."

Phlager asked what I meant, and I told him that Swift had appeared to recognize me when I first talked to him, but then started reciting the old rhyme about the monkey and the elephant when I asked about Shiu.

Phlager didn't know what rhyme I meant, so I started, "I went to the animal fair . . ." If it had been a cartoon, the artist would have drawn a light bulb over Phlager's head.

"Did that seem to be his answer when you asked where Shiu had gone?"

"Yeah. Some answer," I said.

"Hell yes," Phlager said. "He may have been telling you just where Shiu went." He reached into his coat, consulted a fat address book and picked up a phone.

"I told you Dennis Touhy had complied a list of SNS property," he said after punching in a number. "I think I remember something from that . . ."

"Dennis? Phlager. Yeah, I know it's the middle of the night. Wake up and listen to me. Do you remember that property list you made in the Sanders case? Yeah, the professor. OK, did I see that one of the items on that list was a game farm or hunting resort up north? It was? Good, now where's the file?"

Phlager hung up and turned to us. "I'm going over to the state office building to meet Touhy and get the property file. I'll run you two home if you want."

On the way home, I asked Phlager if he thought the file would provide anything important.

"Bob, I don't have any idea. From what I was told, the helicopter was last seen heading north. It may be nothing . . . and it may be the break we've been looking for all week."

"Wait a minute, Bill. Are you talking about Shiu or Frank Sanders?"

"Both, I hope," Phlager said. "We probably should have made the connection and checked out the game farm days ago."

"I don't give a shit about Shiu, but if you think this might have something to do with Frank, I want to know," I said. "Liz and I have gone along with you on this, and I think we're entitled. Certainly she is."

Phlager was quiet for a moment. "OK. You'll know. But there may be no connection."

We got to bed at 2:30 and enjoyed a fine four hours of sleep. Phlager sounded wide awake when I mumbled hello into the phone at 6:30.

"We may have something, Bob. The sheriff up in Coulee County reported to the FAA late last night that a couple of moonlight fishermen on one of the lakes reported seeing a huge, low-flying aircraft headed north . . . in a line for that SNS-owned game farm. They recognized it as a 'copter, but thought it might have been in trouble because it was flying so low.

"I just talked to the sheriff about the game farm. He said it had been out of operation for more than a year, but was used occasionally for hunting and fishing. He said one of his deputies had mentioned that someone apparently had moved into the place last week.

"So, Larry Creston and I are flying up as soon as the state plane can get here."

Now I was wide awake. "Bill, if there's the least chance Frank is up there, Liz and I want to come."

"I don't know. We're not supposed to give reporters rides in state aircraft."

"Oh, come on, the governor does it all the time and so does the adjutant general in National Guard planes. Besides, both of us are material witnesses in a major case."

"Oh, boy, another press table lawyer. All right, Bob, the plane is supposed to be here by eight. If you can be at the airport by then, you both can come."

I rousted Liz out of bed and called a cab. We were on the way to the airport by 7:30 and even had time for coffee and doughnuts before the six-seat state propjet swooshed in.

Creston didn't look too happy about taking civilians along, but Phlager soothed him by telling us that he was letting us come on the express condition that we accept any restrictions on our movement imposed by him or Creston. We hadn't agreed to anything, but kept quiet to avoid queering the deal.

Coulee County was way up in the deep woods in the far northwest corner of the state. The only place that could be called a town was Winston Lakes, and after nearly an hour of flying, we spotted its one-runway airport carved out of the trees. An easy landing, provided the wind was blowing the right way, the pilot told us over his shoulder. He brought us in smoothly, although we got a very close look at the huge pines at the end of the runway.

The sheriff was Grover Reed, and he was decked out in full dress uniform when he greeted us at the tiny terminal. The gray and black tunic and gray pants pressed to a knife-edge crease weren't his workaday clothes—if the cleaning tag he had missed on the coat sleeve was any clue. Reed was a short man gone to fat, but light on his small feet—probably was once a good dancer—maybe even a boxer when he was younger. He had a small oval face and almond-shaped eyes.

"Welcome, all," Reed said as we climbed out of the plane. "I'm afraid I didn't know there was going to be four of you . . ." He gestured toward a pickup truck parked behind the low chain link fence next to the cinderblock terminal.

Liz and Phlager rode into town in the cab with Reed. Creston, looking sour, and I shared a rolled-up tarp in the truck box. I didn't think conversation would be welcome.

We finished our bumpy ride in a crowded county courthouse parking lot. There were three sheriff's cars and four state police sedans and station wagons filling most of the spaces. About twenty uniformed men were leaning against hoods and fenders, sipping coffee, and talking idly.

The sheriff ushered us into a two-room suite in the basement of the old red brick courthouse. He offered us coffee, rousted a young woman in jeans and flannel shirt out of the seat in front of the radio console to get doughnuts, and pulled four chairs into his cubbyhole office.

"Haven't had this many visitors since the old senator came

up to hunt deer and shot Marshall Barker's prize bull," he said. He looked around, pausing his gaze on Liz.

Phlager picked up on it. "Miss Sanders's father is the man who vanished from the university," he said. "She may be able to help. This is her friend, Mr. Wartovsky."

The sheriff decided there was nothing he could do about it. He stood up and turned to a map in back of his desk.

"The game farm is up here on Lac du Sac," he said, pointing to an irregular blue blob in the northeast corner of the map. "About thirty miles from the county seat here."

He picked up a broad sheet from the desk and turned it toward us. "This is the township map." The lake was shaped like a riverboat captain's whiskey decanter—fat and oblong at the bottom with a long narrow neck. Right where the cork would go there was an elongated area of land—an island that looked as if it must be no more than a long stone's throw from the shore.

Pointing to the top of the neck, he said, "The place is here. They have all the land along the shore to where the lake widens out and about half a mile back. It's second-growth . . . thick woods. The buildings are on the island, connected by a wooden bridge you can walk across, but too narrow for a car. There's one dirt road in . . . about two miles off the county hardtop. Also, it's been dry as hell, and anything on wheels will raise dust you can see a couple miles."

"Can we go in through the trees?" Creston asked.

"I don't know," the sheriff said. "I sent Russell . . . Russell Lafever . . . up this morning to look. If anybody can get in quiet, it's old Russell. Real woodsy fella. Folks say he can sneak up and goose a bear . . ." Reed looked at Liz and flushed red. "Ah, well. He ought to be calling in soon. Good, here's Mary Louise with the doughnuts."

We poured more coffee and munched the doughnuts. After about forty minutes the telephone rang, and Mary Louise waved the receiver through the open door at the sheriff. "Deppity Lafever," she said.

The sheriff punched a button and picked up his phone. "Russell? How come you didn't use the radio? Oh. Yeah." He scribbled on a scratch pad and listened for about ten minutes without commenting and then said, "Where? OK, Russell, we'll meet you on the county road at the Exxon. About eleven I guess."

He hung up and turned to us, glancing at his notes. "The helicopter is there—parked out on the far end of the island. Russell says he came out to phone because he was afraid they might be monitoring the radio. He got through the woods OK and checked the place out with field glasses. But he says that dirt road is powder . . . taking cars in would be like phoning to say we're comin'.

"Oh, and he says there are three people out there. A little guy and a big bruiser were fooling around with the 'copter. Both carrying guns. Third was a tall man, kind of heavy, in one of the animal cages. Says he fits the description of the kidnapped guy."

"In a cage?" Liz gasped.

"Big open wire cages they had there for the animals they used to keep for breeding," the sheriff said. "Russell says he looked OK—kind of ragged—but walking around and fit enough.

"He says the cages are pretty exposed and would be between us and the lodge if we went in over the bridge. About the only safe way would be to somehow warn the guy in the cage to lay low."

"That's a problem," Creston said. "If that's Sanders, we can't go in there with him in the line of fire. And how the hell could we warn him we're coming?"

"Bird calls," Liz said. Everyone looked at her.

"Daddy and I used to play Indians when I was little. He taught me bird calls he said the Indians used to signal each other. There was one, the mourning dove, I think, for 'help on the way,' and another for 'hide.' That was the towhee call."

"The towhee?" I asked.

"A rare bird, but a distinctive call," Liz said. She looked at Phlager. "I could warn him."

"Out of the question," Creston said. "Bill, I'm not taking any civilians into a potential fire fight."

Phlager stood up. "Let's go out there and look it over. I agree with you about jeopardizing civilians, Larry, but you know very well there are some times when you can't avoid it. Sending them out with ransom money for one thing. Wiring them to get evidence for another. So let's just play it by ear, OK?"

Creston nodded unhappily and we trooped out to the cars. Liz and I rode with Phlager in a state car. Creston was with the sheriff.

The county road was winding, but relatively well maintained, and the motorcade encountered no traffic. We pulled up to a combination filling station-general store at a crossroads after a forty-five minute ride. A huge, black-bearded man, wearing a plaid shirt over pin-striped trousers held up by red suspenders, was standing beside a jeep. He had field glasses around his neck and a rifle in a sling on his back.

Deputy Lafever spoke briefly to the sheriff as Creston and Phlager listened. He pointed to the thick woods across the road from the station and then cocked his head as Reed spoke. The sheriff turned to point at Liz, and Lafever's beard opened in a big-toothed grin. He waved us over to the group.

"Missy, you can sing like the towhee?"

Liz smiled and warbled a bird call.

"Damn if that isn't it. Heard 'em lots, but never could pick it up," Lafever said. He turned to the sheriff. "There's plenty of cover up to the shore. I could take her in and get her in a safe place before we move. It sure makes our chances of giving that fella a chance to get out of the way a lot better. I don't know no better way, anyhow."

The sheriff looked at Creston, who nodded curtly. Lafever stepped over to the knot of county and state policemen. He picked three of the deputies to lead groups through the woods and sketched on the dusty ground a quick map of the routes they should follow.

When he finished, the sheriff said, "This has got to go down just right. Morris and Jake, you going to be on opposite sides of the island, so be damn sure you ain't so far down the shoreline that if there's shooting you have to fire straight across and maybe hit each other. Get yourselves at an angle to the lodge so the guns are pointed out towards the lake. Me and Willie will go down the road.

"There's a man down there in one of their animal cages . . . he's the subject we're tryin' to rescue. Russell here is taking a party in that will try to alert him to hide or get low. Watch for him to move . . . that's when we'll show ourselves on the road. If the man don't get the message, we'll go anyway, but for God's sake don't fire near him or from anyplace that would put him in the line of return fire."

The sheriff was carrying a battery-powered megaphone. "We'll give them one warning on the bullhorn as soon as everybody's ready on the shore. Stay in cover till we see what they do or till our group starts over the bridge. No shooting unless they fire first. But if they do, I want a hellacious crossfire from you all.

"Now, test the walkies before we leave. Don't use 'em till you're in position and then just two words—'Ready, Morris,' 'Ready, Jake,' 'Ready, Willie.' Don't break cover till you've heard the other two, but watch the bridge close in case you miss a transmission or the radios fuck up. As soon as we get across the bridge, Morris and Jake, each of you send three men down the shoreline back to the bridge to back us up. Once we go, the radios are open."

The policemen opened the car trunks and unloaded an arsenal; automatic rifles, gas grenade launchers, and a couple of those big-bore hunting guns that are supposed to be able to drop a rhino.

Five men each formed up behind Morris and Jake and

slanted off into the woods in opposite directions. Creston and the sheriff went with the deputy called Willie and about eight men to a narrow dirt road about fifty yards down the county highway. In two groups they walked single file down the grassy shoulders.

Liz, Phlager, and I followed Lafever straight across the road and into the trees. It was amazing to watch the big deputy picking his way through the forest, detouring around the worst thickets, and leading us with little difficulty through what seemed to be solid stands of massed trees. None of us were outfitted for the terrain by L. L. Bean standards, but except for a few aggressive thorn bushes and a couple of marshy spots, we made our way without getting ourselves or our clothes noticeably torn or soiled.

We moved quickly for about half an hour to a small clearing. Lafever motioned us to stop and in a low voice said, "I figger we got about a quarter mile more to the lake. From here on, everybody got to walk careful. We don't want nobody taking a fall or cracking branches. And no talking a'tall. Watch for me to signal where to walk and what to do."

With the careful movement, it was another twenty minutes, but at last Lafever stopped and raised his hand. He vanished into the brush for about five minutes, reappeared and motioned us to go down to hands and knees. With Liz behind him and Phlager and I following, he crawled into a clump of bushes.

After about twenty yards, we stopped behind the huge root ball of a fallen tree. We were about ten feet from the edge of the lake and through the tangle of dirt-encrusted roots we could see the island about thirty yards out in the water.

The island looked to be about one hundred yards long, maybe thirty—forty across. Three wire cages, each about eight feet high and about ten feet wide and long, were under the trees just across from our hiding place. Beyond them, maybe forty yards, was a low-lying log building. There was some kind of string or wire stretched from the center cage to the building, looped through a window. The door facing us was open and the faint sound of a radio could be heard.

At the far end of the island was an open field. The helicopter, looking like a gigantic mechanical grasshopper, was hunkered down in the grass. Farther on, where the island was closest to the wide part of the lake, there was a dock with a boat—outboard, it looked like—bobbing on the end of a rope.

The narrow wooden bridge to the island was on our right about twenty yards. A car was parked in a small cleared area where the road came out of the woods.

At first, I didn't see anyone in the cages, but a movement in the center enclosure caught my eye. A man was sitting on the ground with his back against the wire, facing the log building. I waved at Lafever and pointed. He nodded and tapped Liz on the shoulder and pointed to the cage. He raised his thumb and forefinger to his lips.

On her knees, Liz gave a cooing bird call. Nothing happened. She did it again and the man started. He clambered to his feet and turned toward the lake, scanning the trees across the narrow strip of water with a puzzled look on his face.

Frank had a pretty good growth of beard, but looked all right. Glancing back toward the cabin occasionally, he continued to search the shoreline. Lafever leaned over and whispered in Liz's ear. She sounded the first call again and then gave the towhee call she had demonstrated for Lafever.

Frank caught on. He yawned elaborately, stretched his arms over his head, and sauntered toward a three-sided wooden enclosure at one end of the cage. He flopped down on a cot against its back wall.

Lafever smiled and patted Liz on the back. He pointed to the gap in the trees where the road ended. The sheriff, with a walkie-talkie to his ear and the megaphone in the other hand, was moving bent over out of the woods, behind the car. Willie was behind him with an automatic rifle.

The sheriff rested the megaphone on the car fender, looked around once, and flicked the switch.

"THIS IS SHERIFF REED." The words boomed out of the megaphone and rolled over the lake. "THE ISLAND IS SURROUNDED. COME OUT INTO OPEN GROUND WITH YOUR HANDS EMPTY AND YOUR ARMS RAISED."

The scene went dead quiet. The radio went off in the lodge. The door swung closed, and a gun barrel appeared at the lower sill of the window facing the bridge.

"THIRTY SECONDS TO COME OUT," the sheriff broadcast. "COME OUT NOW AND NO ONE WILL GET HURT."

The response was a shot that ripped into the side window of the car to the left of the sheriff. Reed ducked back and Willie, kneeling by the front bumper, let off a fusillade of shots that sent wood chips flying around the window frame. Inside, something made of glass shattered.

On the shoreline on each side of the island, the heavily armed deputies and troopers thrashed out of the woods and found cover behind fallen trees. The sheriff was talking rapidly into his radio. He poked the megaphone over the car hood again.

"THAT'S IT IN THERE. SURRENDER NOW OR WE'LL BLOW THAT CABIN APART!"

Another shot came from the lodge. Reed spoke into the radio again, and gunfire poured into the cabin from three sides as Willie's squad moved into position. In the cage, Frank slid off the cot against the back wall of the shed and pulled the mattress over him.

More silence. Then a door slammed at the rear of the lodge and a squat figure scuttled out in a zigzagging run toward the helicopter. Three more shots were fired from the front window and another salvo was returned from the opposite shore, chewing up the cabin and raising puffs of grass and dirt behind the running figure of Shiu. The range was long and he was moving like a combat veteran.

Shiu reached the helicopter and clambered into the cabin. A coughing sound came out of the rotor engine. Reed yelled into the radio, and several deputies from Jake's group ran down the shoreline to get into position directly across from the parked aircraft.

Kenny Kehler, carrying a carbine with a long, curved magazine protruding from the bottom, bolted out of the back door of the lodge, heading for the 'copter. Reed waved at Willie, who pounded across the bridge with his entire squad behind him.

Lafever handed me his glasses, jumped out onto the shore and ran toward the bridge. Phlager, Liz, and I followed. On the island, she and I turned toward the cage where Frank was sitting up behind his mattress. Lafever and Phlager followed the running lawmen toward the end of the island.

The cage was secured with a railroad spike dropped through two eyebolts on the gate and the cage frame. I jerked it out and Liz ran to Frank, who got up and hugged her, grinning. In the direction of the lodge, I heard what sounded like a doorbell ringing. With Liz wrapped around him, Frank gave me a thumbs up gesture with a free hand.

I decided to leave them alone and left the cage, trotting to the corner of the lodge, where I could watch the action in what I hoped was relative safety. Inside the lodge, the doorbell rang insistently.

Out in the field, a high whine came from the helicopter, and its giant rotor blades began swinging slowly. Kehler was about fifty feet from the big machine when it suddenly lurched off the ground. Willie and his men were making up ground fast.

Even over the motor, I could hear Kehler scream, "Shiu, you bastard, wait!" as the 'copter bucked and jerked in the air about eight feet off the ground. The wash from the rotors plastered his clothes against his body.

Shiu poked his head out of the window and waved toward the lake. The helicopter rose another twenty-five feet and slid crablike toward the end of the island. Jake's men were beginning to fire at both the 'copter and at Kehler. Willie's group was within fifty yards and closing.

Kehler looked around wildly and ran for the dock at the end of the island. Shiu had guided the helicopter about one hundred yards past the shore, where it hovered about thirty feet above the surface, roiling the water. Kehler reached the dock and vaulted into the boat. He tore the mooring line free, leaned over the big outboard motor, and snapped the cord. The motor roared and the boat bounced off the dock's pilings and headed out into the lake.

Willie and one of his deputies reached the dock. Willie fired at the helicopter; the other man at the boat. Kehler, bent over the steering handle of the engine, suddenly jerked upright and screamed. Through the glasses I could see a red stain soaking through the back of his shirt.

The boat was directly under the helicopter. Kehler struggled to stand astride the seats, but fell back. Shiu tried to lower the helicopter to water level, but could not match his movements with the boat's erratic course changes as Kehler groped for the steering handle.

After several tries, a couple bullets plunked into the side of the helicopter. Shiu looked out of the side window and shouted something that was lost in all the noise. He began pulling the 'copter up and away from the boat.

Kehler stood again—this time with the carbine in his hands. He shrieked something at the helicopter, waving the carbine wildly. As the huge aircraft moved steadily away from him, Kehler unloaded the gun into its underside.

The salvo hit either Shiu or the 'copter controls. The ungainly machine bucked violently and threw its tail up.

A puff of flame shot out the side of the helicopter, and the cabin disappeared in a black and yellow ball of smoke and fire. Flaming fragments catapulted out across the lake, sizzling into the water. The largest intact section, the forward third of the fuselage, plummeted downward. It smashed into the boat and carried it steaming under the water.

The deputies, guns lowered, stood watching the bubbles break the surface. Across the water, a trilling song came out of the silent woods. I wondered if Liz knew what bird it was.

CHAPTER 17

The sheriff, Creston, and about half the men who had taken part in the operation remained at the game farm, searching the lodge and combing the grounds from the bridge to the dock, looking for God knows what. Probably just to have something to do until boats and scuba equipment could be brought in for what was going to be the nasty job of recovering the bodies.

One of the state police station wagons was driven in to the lake, and a mattress and blankets brought from the lodge to be laid out in the back, but Frank refused to lie down.

"Come on, people, I'm OK. I've been eating regular and 'cept for this beard, I've even been keeping clean. Probably healthier for sleeping outdoors in my cage."

Frank rode out sitting between Liz and me with Phlager riding up front with the state trooper driver. Frank insisted that he be brought up to date on everything that had happened at the *CR&P* "while I was out of touch," and Liz and I took turns filling in the gaps for him. He laughed uproariously at Liz's description of the concert and the immediate aftermath, but shook his head when I told him about the effect on Swift.

"He really was a hell of a newsman, you know," Frank said. "In another time—eighty, ninety years ago—he might have been in the company of the editors who invented mass circulation newspapers in this country." He paused. "On the other hand, he was wound so tight he might have flipped his wig anyway."

Curiously, Frank also seemed saddened by what had happened to Kehler.

"It's funny . . . maybe it's that syndrome that they've found in hostages who get to feeling sorry for the people who've hijacked their planes or whatever. But really, Kenny wasn't that nasty to me and after a couple of days we got along pretty well," Frank said.

"It's fairly common," Phlager said. "Kidnap victims, especially if they're treated halfway decently, sometimes will come back and talk sympathetically about their kidnappers. I've even heard of political hostages who support their captors' causes after they're released.

"There's guilt, too, if you can imagine it. People who've been in hijackings will sometimes come back sounding like it was somehow all their fault for using that airline or taking that flight—almost as if they believe it wouldn't have happened if they hadn't been there."

"Oh, yes, guilt," Frank said. "I spent most of my time in that damn cage thinking how dumb I had been—how I invited what happened."

"Invited it?" Liz asked. "How, Daddy?"

"Wishful thinking. Bob told me that Swift had recognized me, and I pretended there would be no problem if I just left town . . . ignoring the obvious likelihood that Swift would tell Shiu—that you would be suspect, Liz—and that when you took up with Bob they would start watching both of you. I should have just bagged it right then . . . told the Center to find someone else for the job.

"But I wanted to do it, and I just ignored the kind of warning flags that in the old days I would have paid attention to. Hell, I forgot elementary stuff like stashing the documents and my notes in a safe place and making backup copies of the stuff. So Kenny got it all from my desk when he grabbed me, and it's all at the bottom of the lake now. I saw them loading the box on the 'copter just before you showed up today.

"But I'm relieved they didn't come after either or both of you when they took me."

"Why didn't they?" I asked.

"I guess because you didn't have the information they wanted kept quiet. Kenny said they had Bob's phone tapped and when he reported our last conversation that night, his boss told him getting me out of circulation ought to take care of the problem."

"Weren't you worried about what they were going to do with you?" Liz asked.

"When he first grabbed me, sure. He caught me coming back from dinner at the faculty club and stuck a gun in my face that looked like something off the battleship *Missouri*. I figured he was going to take me out in the country and put a bullet behind my ear. I kept remembering all the stories I covered about hoods who were found in the Jersey swamps, and how many times I wrote about 'gangland-style killings.'

"But, you know, it became clear quickly that Kenny had been told I wasn't to be harmed. From the first, when he came up behind me outside my apartment, he kept telling me that I wouldn't be hurt if I did what he told me. He spent a lot of time tying and untying me those first hours, and he even asked me a couple of times if the ropes hurt, or if I could breathe all right with the gag in my mouth.

"And, it all turned out OK," Frank said. He smiled and turned to Liz beside him on the back seat.

"Lord, was I surprised to hear you give the towhee call, honey. But what was the mourning dove for?"

Liz's eyes widened. "What was it for? That was the signal for 'help coming,' Daddy."

Frank laughed. "Well, I'm glad you remembered the right one for 'hide.' The meadowlark was the rescue signal, Liz. The mourning dove call meant, 'The white man's horses have been driven off.'"

Phlager asked Frank if he felt up to giving a statement when we got back to Winston Lakes or whether he would prefer to wait until he got back to the university.

"Now's as good a time as any, I guess," Frank said.

The sheriff had alerted Mary Louise by radio, and when we got to Winston Lakes she had rounded up the only steno-typist in the county and cleared the sheriff's desk. She said a number of calls had come in from newspapers and television stations in the area and from wire services in the city.

"They all have police radio scanners, you know," she said. "What should I be telling them, Mr. Phlager?"

"That Sheriff Reed will get back to them," Phlager said.

Frank used the sheriff's department locker room to shower and shave, and Liz went out to see if she could buy him some clean clothes. I phoned the *CR&P*—not knowing if I would even get an answer from a paper whose editor had gone 'round the bend last night and whose publisher had gone down in flames this afternoon.

But Grace picked up the phone, sounding cheery. When I told him where I was, he was excited.

"Listen, what the hell is going on up there? Mooniman got a tip that the state police radio was full of transmissions that sounded like some kind of war up in Coulee County. Dick says one of the old-timers who hangs around the cop house said it sounded like the time some small town cops got into a shoot-out with the Dillinger gang at little Bohemia, Wisconsin. But the wire services haven't had a damn thing except advisories saying they are trying to get the story."

"Well, I've got it and it was a sure-enough shoot-out," I said. "Listen, I'm short of time, so let me dictate a story on what happened, and then I'll call back with more details if I have some."

I gave Grace about two columns on the game farm show-down and thought while I was dictating Swift would have loved it. "Terror in the North Woods," or maybe "Blazing Guns; Watery Grave."

Before hanging up, I asked Grace who was running the paper.

"Fargo's back in charge. He showed up in the newsroom this afternoon and told us he was under instructions to take over temporarily. He said there would be an announcement from the owners 'clarifying the situation' some time today or tomorrow at the latest."

A considerably fresher-looking Frank, wearing jeans and a flannel shirt Liz had brought back, was seated in the sheriff's office sipping coffee when I finished the call. I filled most of a legal pad with notes while he talked and the stenotypist plinked away.

He told the story in detail: being grabbed in front of his apartment building, trussed up while Kehler methodically searched the apartment, being allowed to answer Liz's phone call with a gun at his head, being led to a car, and the long trip to the game farm.

The first night, Kehler let him stay in the lodge. Frank waited until Kenny fell asleep and attempted to sneak out, but Kehler woke up and caught him.

"He tied me up again and the next morning ordered me to take a cot and mattress into one of the animal cages. Said he didn't want to keep me tied, but the cage was the only place he could put me if I wasn't. He couldn't find a padlock, so he rigged up a doorbell that rang in the lodge when the cage door was opened. Kenny was a pretty good handyman as it turned out," Frank said.

He stayed in the cage except for trips to the toilet. Twice when Kehler took him into the lodge and tied him to the bed, he went somewhere in the car.

"Once he came back with provisions but had none the second time, and I think he must have gone somewhere to telephone for instructions. He told me to get used to the place because we might be there a couple of weeks."

But Frank said that night Shiu brought the helicopter to the island, and made several attempts that looked like he was going into the lake until Kehler marked off the landing area with some gas lanterns. "God, was that a hairy landing. But the little bastard really could fly."

The next day the rescue party arrived.

At that point, Phlager asked Frank if he could describe in any detail the material Kehler had taken from his apartment.

Sanders looked at me and answered, "Well, I guess Bob must have told you I was investigating the ownership of the newspaper for the Center for Inquiry in New York. The stuff Kehler got was everything I had collected. Some good evidence, I think. Now, I reckon anything I tell you is just hearsay and speculation."

"Well, don't worry about that, professor," Phlager said. "That's most of the information gathered in any criminal investigation. We've got some documentary evidence ourselves that may duplicate what you lost."

He paused and looked at me in the corner of the room. "Are you worried about being quoted? I suppose we could ask Bob and Miss Sanders to step outside. . . ."

"Throw out reporters?" Frank replied. "My God, no. I'd never be able to live with myself. But, Bob, remember, there's no way right now to back up everything I say.

"The information and the documents I had showed that the newspaper had been purchased by Gene Bright through a dummy holding company. And he never intended to run a legitimate business . . . this was a multimillion-dollar extortion scheme."

"Extortion?" Phlager asked. "Now that's a new wrinkle on this business."

"Let me give you some background," Frank said. "This whole thing was a double-cover operation . . . and a double cross of Granville Swift."

"Swift wasn't in on it?" Phlager asked. "How the hell could he not be?"

"Oh, sure, Swift came up with the original idea of getting control of a small town paper close to big cities and turning it into a sensational tabloid," Frank said.

"He was sure he could produce a daily paper loaded with crime, sex, and 'people' news that could preempt the suburban supermarket base of the weekly tabloids and cut into the home delivery circulation of the stodgier metropolitan dailies. He figured once he established the paper's sales appeal, the big retailers would be easy marks to sell advertising. And since that would be a hell of a threat to the big dailies, the plan had to be kept secret when they first moved in on the small town paper—so that was the first cover.

"Swift couldn't find any regular publisher willing to take a flyer on his scheme and he ended going to Gene Bright. Bright agreed to invest enough in the idea to test it in several markets and brought Shiu, who was known to the mob from his drug traffic days in the Far East, into the project.

"Shiu was installed as publisher, but his real role was to set up a system to airlift the paper to suburban shopping center parking lots. They bought the big helicopter and the containers Bob spotted in the *CR&P* motor pool compound to get the papers down to the lots in the middle of the night. From there they would be distributed to stores and coin vending boxes by Bright's own trucking company."

I wasn't supposed to be a part of the process, but without thinking, I interrupted.

"Wait a minute. How did Kehler figure in?"

Phlager gave me an annoyed look, but Frank answered anyway.

"Kenny had been Bright's flunky for years. Gene sent him to keep an eye on the project . . . and later watch out for Kirk Bright, Gene's son.

"I was told by several sources, including Kenny, that Kirk knew his old man had an interest in the newspaper, but not much else. It was his mother who insisted the kid be given a job and Kenny confirmed that he was told to keep him in the dark. From what he said, Gene was not delighted to have the kid there, but gave in to momma. Kenny said, 'You know what it's like being married to one of these broads.'"

That raised Liz's feminist hackles. "Now, what does that mean?"

"Please," Phlager said. "Let's just try to get a semicoherent record here without a lot of byplay. Professor Sanders, you said there was a double cross involved."

"I'm getting to it. The paper was bought and its style and format changed. The last tip I got before Kenny so rudely interrupted my labors was that they were all set to begin delivering ten thousand papers daily to at least five shopping centers in the suburbs of two cities. The first deliveries were scheduled for the beginning of the month, which I guess would have been next week."

Frank got up and poured himself another cup of coffee.

"Bright did intend to start the deliveries, but a source, who is pretty close to the mob, told me it never was his intention to operate a newspaper for any length of time even if Swift's idea was working. The goodies were just too slow coming in; he wanted a quick cash in.

"You see, Bright was on his way out. To the new young guys he was just another Mustache Pete . . . out of date and in the way. But they wanted a nice quiet retirement—no bloodshed. So when Gene insisted on one last big hit, they set him up with the cash. They put in a couple million for the *Capital Register & Press* and the new equipment and gave him a year to pull off his plan.

"It was simple. There are four major dailies in the two areas he was going to hit. He was going to demonstrate to the publishers that the *CR&P* could cut into their valuable suburban circulation and major advertising.

"When he had made his point, he was going to approach the publishers with an offer to discontinue operations on their turfs for five million bucks each. Then he would have his holding company announce that the project had proven economically impractical and nobody—especially the newspapers that had paid him off—would be likely to ask any embarrassing questions."

Phlager started to interrupt: "But why wouldn't the city papers blow the whistle . . . oh, I see."

"Sure," Frank said. "It was a potentially foolproof racket

because the victims themselves would be involved in illegal or at least unethical conduct, conspiring to restrain competition.

"Bright planned to sell the *CR&P*, figuring lots of chains would be happy to bid for a monopoly newspaper in a state capital, and pay back what the mob had advanced him. So he'd come out with at least twenty million in the clear to take care of himself in his declining years. Kenny sort of confirmed this, too. He said this was his last job and that he would get a big payoff if everything went off right."

"But what about Shiu and Swift?" Phlager asked.

"Shiu was in on the whole thing and also was going to have a chunk of the shakedown money. Swift was going to be left hanging out to dry—mainly because they were pretty sure he wouldn't go along with the real plan. But Bright couldn't dump Swift because he didn't have anyone else to produce a newspaper that would be a credible threat to the publishers he intended to squeeze."

Frank gestured palms up, signifying he was finished.

"Okay, that'll be all," Phlager told the stenotypist.

Liz got up and went over to her father. "I still don't see why you think they didn't intend to hurt you. You knew all about their plans."

"They knew I was on to the first part—moving in on the suburbs. But they had no way of knowing I had wind of the shakedown plan. I think they were just going to cut me loose out in the woods somewhere and be long gone before I told what I did know."

"Well, we may be able to reconstruct the case with what we have and with your help," Phlager said. "What's there to stop Bright from finding himself another Swift and another Shiu and trying again to pull this off?"

Frank smiled. "I really doubt it. My source said some of the boys who bankrolled Bright never did like the idea. I think this was Gene's last fling. With what happened in the last couple of days, he'll be lucky if they don't retire him in the old-fashioned way . . . a trip to the river in a gunny sack with some concrete blocks to keep him company."

In the corner, I riffled through the fat sheaf of notes. "Christ, what am I gonna do with all this?"

Frank came over and put his hand on my shoulder. "You're going to use your experience and judgment, Bob. You've got a story, but you've got to write it in a way that makes clear what happened without giving anybody an open-and-shut libel case. My question is whether your paper will print it. If not, as I suspect, I know some newspapers back East that will."

Mary Louise came in to tell Phlager that the pilot of the state plane had called to say we ought to be leaving as soon as possible because a cold front was kicking off some rough weather. It might make for a bumpy trip and difficult landing if we didn't get ahead of it.

"Half an hour, Bob. I don't want to get stuck here," Phlager said.

I called Grace again and gave him additional details about the kidnapping, including that the motive was to keep Sanders from disclosing information he had gathered in an investigation on behalf of a private foundation.

"What was he investigating, Bob?" Grace asked. "We ought to have something in here about that."

"Jesus, Bill, he was investigating us. The *CR&P*. Swift and Shiu and the people they worked for. He got it all, but the proof is gone and we'd be going way out on a limb if we use it."

"Now you know why I just as soon be a noncom instead of an officer around here," Grace said. "You better talk to Fargo."

Ah, the original gutless wonder, I thought as I waited for Fargo to come on the line. He listened to what I had to say without interruption.

"Bob, we can't print it the way Professor Sanders gave it without something to back us up, but this is damned impor-

tant stuff and we can't ignore it either." I could hear Fargo
take a deep breath.

"Let's do this. Give Grace an insert saying the investigation Sanders was conducting also was the subject of official
scrutiny by the attorney general's office—and that it had to
do with the management and ownership of the *Register &
Press*. Say no charges of criminal activity were pending, but
such action was possible in the course of further investigation."

It was more than I expected from Fargo. "You'll print
that?" I asked.

"Damn right, Bob. I'm no crusader, but if we can't do that
much, maybe it would be a good idea if this paper went
belly up."

After finishing with the story, I rode to the airport with
Phlager, Frank, and Liz, feeling better about Fargo and the
paper. There were thunderheads in the distance as we drove
onto the tarmac, and Liz leaned over and said, "Sit next to
me on the plane." I thought she wanted to hold hands if we
got into bumpy weather.

We were off the ground and heading south in minutes.
The flight plan was to go first to the university town, drop off
Frank and then go on to the capital.

Liz and I were in the rear seats; Frank and Phlager immediately behind the pilot. Liz was quiet for about ten minutes
and then looked at me with a serious expression.

"Bob, I told you that you would never have to guess about
us. I wanted to talk to you about this before, but Daddy's
kidnapping and all the stuff at the paper . . . there just
didn't seem to be a good time."

Suddenly the feeling of contentment I had been feeling
vanished.

"I'm not going back to the capital with you. I'm getting off
with Daddy."

I smiled. "Sure, honey, I understand if you want to be
with him for a while."

"It's more than that, Bob. I'm not coming back to the paper. I went by the journalism school last week while I was in town, and one of the profs mentioned that there was a part-time photographer's job coming open at the *Chicago Tribune*. He suggested I apply. I wrote and there was a reply in the mail yesterday. I can have the job if I want it."

"How about school? Don't you want to get your degree?"

"Yes, and the *Trib* is willing to work my hours around classes at Northwestern. Bob, I don't want to leave you, but this is the kind of chance that doesn't come along often."

I felt like telling her she was a chance for me that might never come along again. Instead, I smiled—bravely, I hope—and said, "Sure, Liz. You can't pass it up. Chicago is a big jump and I'd take it in a minute."

"We'll see each other," she said. "It's not a long trip. You can come down on weekends. Or I can come up."

"Sure."

We chatted lightly the rest of the trip, and Liz gave me a long, lingering kiss before she clambered out of the plane behind Frank. We took off immediately.

I moved up beside Phlager. "You look down," he said. "Reaction to the day?"

"Just tired, Bill. I'm getting a little long in the tooth to be a combat correspondent."

"Sure," Phlager said. Actually, he was the one who hadn't slept in two days. After a few minutes his head went forward and he was out for the rest of the trip.

The weather had followed us into the capital and we came down just as big drops began pelting the runway. It was pouring by the time we pulled up to the state hangar.

Two cars were waiting for us. Phlager's wife was in one; Fargo Barton in the other. He waved at me as we sprinted for the cover of the hangar. I ran to his car and jumped into the passenger seat.

"I thought you might need a ride," Fargo said as he moved the car away from the hangar.

We rode a few minutes in silence. Fargo began talking as he looked straight ahead into the downpour.

"We got the news about the paper just after you called from up north," he said. "A lawyer from *All-American Enterprises* called and said they had decided . . . what did he say? . . . 'phase out the corporation's commitments in the print environment and concentrate on the ephemeral media.' Anyway, we've been sold again."

"Oh, who . . ."

"He told me the new ownership wants to retain the present staff setup for now," Fargo said. He gave me a quick glance. "Of course, we need a new managing editor. I suggested you."

"Me? How about you? Or Grace?"

"I haven't got the stomach for it, Bob. You can't do the job if it takes you twenty-eight years to get up the courage to make a decision that ought to come instinctively. And Bill just doesn't want to be anything except what he already is. The job is yours if you'll take it."

I surprised myself. "Damn right I'll take it."

I found myself thinking about how we could cover the primary, which was coming up Tuesday, and start showing this could be a good paper—responsible, interesting, maybe even exciting. Not much time—better get at it today.

Fargo was smiling. "Good. I think you'll do a good job. You know, Swift told me a couple of months ago that he thought you had the fiber to be a cracking good editor. Sounded like he was talking about a cereal."

"Wait a minute. You didn't say who bought the paper."

"Oh," Fargo said. He took one hand off the steering wheel and groped in his coat pocket. "I'wrote it down. Got it here somewhere. I couldn't quite place the fellow's name, but Claggett recognized it right off. An Australian, I think he said."